"Hi." The recept... voice she asked, "How can I help you?"

"I'm with Eternal . . . um . . . Burns Funeral Home in Sleepy Hollow, Kentucky. I need to talk to Emmitt Moss about a client of ours. Mamie Sue Preston." I didn't feel one bit bad for lying.

Mamie Sue might be hiding something from me and it might not have to do with her murder, but now my curiosity was up. Which was not a good thing. A southern woman always wanted to be seen as a lady, but really, we were all nosy.

She held a finger in the air and jumped out of her seat.

"Hold on," she quipped. A wary, haunted look crossed her eyes before she rushed down the hall and into a room.

A few seconds later she and a stocky older man in a black suit with a nicely manicured goatee emerged from the room.

He looked at me, said a couple words in the woman's ear, and gestured for me to come on back.

By Tonya Kappes

Ghostly Southern Mystery Series

A GHOSTLY UNDERTAKING • A GHOSTLY GRAVE
A GHOSTLY DEMISE • A GHOSTLY MURDER

Olivia Davis Paranormal Mystery Series

SPLITSVILLE.COM • COLOR ME LOVE
COLOR ME A CRIME

Magical Cures Mystery Series

A CHARMING CRIME • A CHARMING CURE
A CHARMING POTION (novella)
A CHARMING WISH • A CHARMING SPELL
A CHARMING SECRET

Grandberry Falls Series

THE LADYBUG JINX • HAPPY NEW LIFE
A SUPERSTITIOUS CHRISTMAS (novella)
NEVER TELL YOUR DREAMS

A Divorced Diva Bending Mystery Series

A BREAD OF DOUBT SHORT STORY
STRUNG OUT TO DIE

Bluegrass Romance Series

GROOMING MR. RIGHT
TAMING MR. RIGHT

Women's Fiction

CARPE BREAD 'EM

TONYA KAPPES

A
GHOSTLY
MURDER

A GHOSTLY SOUTHERN MYSTERY

WITNESS

An Imprint of HarperCollinsPublishers

WITNESS

An Imprint of HarperCollins*Publishers*
195 Broadway
New York, New York 10007

Copyright © 2015 by Tonya Kappes
Excerpts from *A Ghostly Undertaking, A Ghostly Grave, A Ghostly Demise* copyright © 2013, 2015 by Tonya Kappes
ISBN 978-0-06-237493-6
www.witnessimpulse.com

To Eddy, Jack, Austin, Brady,
Linda and John Robert Lowry, Tracy,
David, Ben and Maddie Darlington.
The loves of my life.

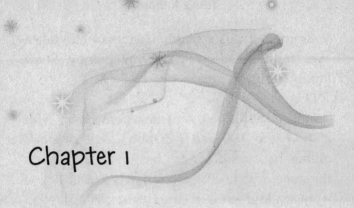

Chapter 1

Ding, ding, ding.

The ornamental bell on an old cemetery headstone rang out. No one touching it. No wind or breeze.

The string attached to the top of the bell hung down the stone and disappeared into the ground. To the naked eye it would seem as though the bell dinged from natural causes, like the wind, but my eye zeroed in on the string as it slowly moved up and down. Deliberately.

I stepped back and looked at the stone. The chiseled words I TOLD YOU I WAS SICK. MAMIE SUE PRESTON were scrolled in fancy lettering. Her date of death was a few years before I took over as undertaker at Eternal Slumber Funeral Home.

Granted, it was a family business I had taken over from my parents and my granny. Some family business.

Ding, ding, ding.

I looked at the bell. A petite older woman, with a short gray bob neatly combed under a small pillbox hat, was doing her best to sit ladylike on the stone, with one leg crossed over the other. She wore a pale green skirt suit. Her fingernail tapped the bell, causing it to ding.

I couldn't help but notice the large diamond on her finger, the strand of pearls around her neck and some more wrapped on her wrist. And with a gravestone like that . . . I knew she came from money.

"Honey child, you can see me, can't you?" she asked. Her lips smacked together. She grinned, not a tooth in her head. There was a cane in her hand. She tapped the stone with it. "Can you believe they buried me without my teeth?"

I closed my eyes. Squeezed them tight. Opened them back up.

"Ta-da. Still here." She put the cane on the ground and tap-danced around it on her own grave.

"Don't do that. It's bad luck." I repeated another Southern phrase I had heard all my life.

She did another little giddy-up.

"I'm serious," I said in a flat, inflectionless voice. "Never dance or walk over someone's grave. It's bad luck."

"Honey, my luck couldn't get any worse than it already is." Her face was drawn. Her onyx eyes set. Her jaw tensed. "Thank Gawd you are here. There is no way I can cross over without my teeth." She smacked her lips. "Oh, by the way, Digger Spears just sent me, and I passed Cephus Hardy on the way. He told me exactly where I could find you."

She leaned up against the stone.

"Let me introduce myself." She stuck the cane in the crook of her elbow and adjusted the pill-box hat on her head. "I'm the wealthiest woman in Sleepy Hollow, Mamie Sue Preston, and I can pay you whatever you'd like to get me to the other side. But first, can you find my teeth?"

I tried to swallow the lump in my throat. This couldn't be happening. Couldn't I have just a few days off between my Betweener clients?

I knew exactly what she meant when she said she needed my help for her cross over, and it wasn't because she was missing her dentures.

"Whatdaya say?" Mamie Sue pulled some cash out of her suit pocket.

She licked her finger and peeled each bill back one at a time.

"Emma Lee," I heard someone call. I turned to see Granny waving a handkerchief in the air and bolting across the cemetery toward me.

Her flaming-red hair darted about like a cardinal as she weaved in and out of the gravestones.

"See," I muttered under my breath and made sure my lips didn't move. "Granny knows not to step on a grave."

"That's about the only thing Zula Fae Raines Payne knows," Mamie said.

My head whipped around. Mamie's words got my attention. Amusement lurked in her dark eyes.

"Everyone is wondering what you are doing clear over here when you are overseeing Cephus Hardy's funeral way over there." Granny took a swig of the can of Stroh's she was holding.

Though our small town of Sleepy Hollow, Kentucky, was a dry county—which meant liquor sales were against the law— I had gotten special permission to have a beer toast at Cephus Hardy's funeral.

I glanced back at the final resting place where everyone from Cephus's funeral was still sitting under the burial awning, sipping on the beer.

"I was just looking at this old stone," I lied.

Mamie's lips pursed suspiciously when she looked at Granny. Next thing I knew, Mamie was sitting on her stone, legs crossed, tapping the bell. *Ding, ding, ding.* "We have a goner who needs help!" Mamie continued to ding the bell. "A goner who is as dead as yesterday." She twirled her cane around her finger.

I did my best to ignore her. If Granny knew I was able to see the ghosts of dead people—not just any dead people, murdered dead people—she'd have me committed for what Doc Clyde called the Funeral Trauma.

A few months ago and a couple ghosts ago, I was knocked out cold from a big plastic Santa that Artie, from Artie's Meat and Deli, had stuck on the roof of his shop during the winter months. It just so happened I was walking on the sidewalk when the sun melted the snow away, sending the big fella off the roof right on top of me. I woke up in the hospital and saw that my visitor was one of my clients—one of my *dead* clients. I thought I was a goner just like him, because my Eternal Slumber clients weren't alive, they were dead, and here was one standing next to me.

When the harsh realization came to me that I wasn't dead and I was able to see dead people, I told Doc Clyde about it. He gave me some little pills and diagnosed me with the Funeral Trauma, a.k.a. a case of the crazies.

He was nice enough to say he thought I had been around dead bodies too long since I had grown up in the funeral home with Granny and my parents.

My parents took early retirement and moved to Florida, while my granny also retired, leaving me and my sister, Charlotte Rae, in charge.

"Well?" Granny tapped her toe and crossed her arms. "Are you coming back to finish the funeral or not?" She gave me the stink-eye, along with a once-over, before she slung back the can and finished off the beer. "Are you feeling all right?"

"I'm feeling great, Zula Fae Raines Payne." Mamie Sue leaned her cane up against her stone. She jumped down and clasped her hands in front of her. She stretched them over her head. She jostled her head side to side. "Much better now that I can move about, thanks to Emma Lee."

Ahem, I cleared my throat.

"Yes." I smiled and passed Granny on the way back over to Cephus Hardy's funeral. "I'm on my way."

"Wait!" Mamie called out. "I was murdered! Aren't you going to help me? Everyone said that you were the one to help me!"

Everyone? I groaned and glanced back.

Mamie Sue Preston planted her hands on her small hips. Her eyes narrowed. Her bubbly personality had dimmed. She'd been dead a long time. She wasn't going anywhere anytime soon, and neither was I.

Chapter 2

"What was going on with you at the cemetery this morning?" Charlotte Rae asked once she pushed open my office door. She leaned on the door frame and tapped the toe of her fancy black high-heeled shoe.

Her long red hair cascaded down the front of her shoulders. Her green eyes bored into me. She drummed her fingers together, tapping her perfectly manicured pink fingernails together. She wore a pair of black slacks, a white blouse and hot pink jewelry to finish off the look.

"Nothing was going on with me," I responded and took my hands out of the filing cabinet. I pushed the drawer back.

There was only one person who knew about my

gift as a Betweener. Sheriff Jack Henry Ross, my boyfriend and Sleepy Hollow's head law enforcer.

I closed the filing cabinet where we kept the files of our clients who were already six feet under.

There wasn't a file anywhere on Mamie Sue Preston. When I had gotten home from sticking Cephus in the ground, I had scoured the funeral-home files in the attic, in the basement, and in my office. There hadn't been any sign of her on paper or in ghost form. She hadn't shown up since I'd seen her near her grave.

"Why are you in the past client files?" Charlotte Rae asked. She walked into my office. Her eyes slid over to the old filing cabinet.

"And it's your business?" I asked.

"We are partners." She reminded me how convenient that word was when she needed it to be.

"You stick with selling the packages and creating new business while I stick with the dead." I grabbed my phone off the desk.

Charlotte Rae and I had one thing in common— our last name. In fact, Charlotte was reluctant to go to mortuary school, while I had been chomping at the bit to get there. When we took over Eternal Slumber after Granny retired, Charlotte made it clear she was in charge of the day-to-day office duties. She met with families, did the interior decorating—you know, the clean, don't-get-your-hands-dirty stuff. The rest was left up to me.

I didn't mind picking up the bodies and making sure the funeral arrangements were in place, everything went smoothly during the service, the gravesite was prepared for burial, the cemetery stone was ordered—the list went on and on.

"Now where are you going?" she asked in a cross tone.

"Do you need me for something?" I asked. The information I needed was not in the cabinet, it was in Granny's head.

"I wanted to make sure you were ready for Junior's funeral."

"Have I ever not been ready?" I asked. There was some reason she was keeping tabs on me, and I wasn't sure what it was.

Charlotte Rae never came into my office. And she never asked where I was going, nor had she ever cared.

"Maybe we can walk down to Higher Grounds Café." She faked a yawn. "I could use an afternoon cup of pick-me-up."

"Nah." I shooed her off and cha-chaed past her, almost knocking into John Howard Lloyd. "Hey, John Howard."

"Afternoon, Emma Lee. Umm . . ." He stalled and looked between me and Charlotte Rae. "Can I have a word with you, ma'am?"

"Sure." I checked the time on my phone. I wanted to get over to Sleepy Hollow Inn to get some answers about Mamie Sue Preston before the Inn guests got restless and wanted dinner.

"Miss Charlotte." John Howard nodded his unruly head of hair and walked past her before she scampered away.

"Thank you," I said for making Charlotte Rae scurry away. She wasn't good with working with the salt-of-the-earth employees at Eternal Slumber.

"For what, ma'am?" John Howard tucked his dirt-stained fingers in the bib of his overalls.

"Nothing." I gestured for him to sit down in one of the chairs in front of my desk.

"How can I help you?" I asked.

"Well . . ." he stalled. "I hate to ask, but—"

"I know, I know," I interrupted. I ran my hands down my dull brown hair and tucked a strand behind my ear. "You do deserve a raise. I know it's hard to be the only employee who digs the graves. Plus you do all the landscaping, which looks great."

I ripped a piece of paper out of the notebook

and grabbed a pen. I scribbled a number on the paper.

"How about this?" I pushed the paper to the edge of the desk.

He eased up on the chair and took a look.

"That's mighty nice of you, Emma Lee." He folded his hands and sat back. "But O'Dell and Bea Allen Burns—"

"Are you telling me that Burns Funeral is already trying to steal you away from me?" I swear smoke was coming out of my ears.

John Howard Lloyd had come to town years ago, needing a job. Granny had given him one with no questions asked. Luckily, he stayed on when Charlotte Rae and I took over. He was the gravedigger and groundskeeper of the funeral home. I'd had no idea that my competitor, Burns Funeral, was trying to steal him away from me.

"Isn't it enough O'Dell just beat Granny in the mayoral election?" I spat. "Since his sister came back to town and started running the funeral home, I'll bet she's after all my employees."

I made a quick mental note to check on the status of all the staff at Eternal Slumber and make sure they were happy with their jobs. Bea Allen Burns hadn't lived in Sleepy Hollow for years. Now that her brother, O'Dell, was the newly elected mayor, she'd decided to stay and run the funeral home while he ran the city.

"Those Burns are not going to take over all of Sleepy Hollow." I grabbed the paper, scribbled out the number and wrote a larger number. "This is it. I can't offer any more money."

I walked around and handed John Howard the piece of paper.

"Golly, Emma Lee." His eyes grew, and he gulped. "I wasn't expecting this. Thank you."

"Good. That's settled." I walked toward the door. "I have to get going. I've got to go see Granny at the Inn."

"But Emma Lee." John Howard stopped me again. "This is a nice raise and I appreciate it, but that's not what I came in here for."

"It's not?" I was a little confused.

"No, ma'am." He slipped the piece of paper in the front pocket of his overalls. "I was just wanting to know if you'd be interested in sponsoring me and a few fellows for the new men's softball league they got going over at the old Softball Junction field."

"Sponsor?" I asked.

"Well, Burns Funeral is going to sponsor a team, and Artie's Meat and Deli is going to sponsor some fellas. And the raise is much appreciated."

He nodded his head. "But we need someone to sponsor us and provide us with things like shirts and stuff."

"What kind of stuff?" I questioned. How was I going to tell Charlotte Rae about the raise—big money—I just spent on keeping John Howard, when he wasn't even planning on leaving?

"Oh goodie!" Mamie Sue appeared. She twirled around with her hands clasped in front of her and smiled. Having no teeth didn't seem to bother her at all. "I loved going to those games! Did you say Softball Junction?"

I had to ignore her so John Howard wouldn't think I was crazy.

"Like gloves, shoes, shirts, balls and fees." He shrugged. "That sort of stuff."

"And Burns is going to have a team?" I asked.

"Take me out to the ball game, take me out with the crowd," Mamie Sue sang off-key as loud as she could. She swayed her cane in the air. "Mmm . . ." She licked her lips. "I love peanuts and Cracker Jacks. Especially those little toys that come in the box. Take me out to the ball game," she sang as loud as she could, placing her hand over her heart. Her pillbox hat shifted slightly to the side. She quickly pushed it back in place.

"Yes, ma'am," he confirmed.

"Okay!" I screamed over Mamie Sue. "Eternal Slumber will sponsor the team. And I'm going to see if Jack Henry wants to play!"

John Howard's eye squinted. He put his finger in his ear and wiggled it.

I had a plan.

"If Burns thinks they are going to beat us on the softball field, they have another thing coming to them!"

Jack Henry had played high school baseball and was pretty good at it. He would be Eternal Slumber's secret weapon against Burns Funeral.

"What is all this screaming about?" Charlotte stormed down the hall and looked into my office.

"Play ball!" Mamie yelled. She swung her cane and pretended to hit an imaginary ball. "Home run!"

I busted in a hysterical fit of laughter.

Both Charlotte Rae and John Howard were staring at me with a slight, watchful hesitation.

"Was I yelling?" I asked in a hushed voice. I got myself together and walked over to the door. "I was checking out the acoustics in here. It's for Junior's funeral tonight. Sometimes it can get loud in here with so many people, and I think we are going to have a big crowd tonight."

Junior Mullins had been the oldest citizen of Sleepy Hollow. He had spent the last part of his life in the nursing home. I was positive the town was going to send him off in style.

"Oh." Charlotte Rae's eyes narrowed before she spun around on the balls of her feet and darted off down the hall.

"So," I whispered and glanced down the hall to make sure Charlotte was back in her office, "is it okay for Jack Henry to join the team?"

"Sure thing, Emma Lee." John Howard walked out of my office with me. "So I can tell the boys you agreed to sponsoring us?"

"Yes, you can." I smiled. There was no way I wasn't going to, even if I had to pay for it out of my own money.

I walked down the hall toward the front of the funeral home and into the vestibule. Velvet curtains hung from each window. I fluffed each one out when I walked by. Dust shot out in clouds.

"Charlotte?" I hollered out. "How long has it been since you cleaned the curtains?"

The click of her heels getting closer made my heart beat a little faster. She peeked her head out of her office door.

"I never agreed to clean them." She drew back. Her lashes batted.

"It's part of your duties to keep the funeral home appealing." I smacked the curtain, and more dust came out. "Yuck."

"You can always call Dixie." Mamie appeared in the chair next to the pedestal where the memorial cards for Junior were located. "I have no idea what she is doing now that I'm dead. Poor Dixie. I hated leaving her. Mind you, it *was* against my will. That is why I'm still here. Remember?" She planted her cane on the hardwood floor and danced a jig around it.

"Emma Lee." Charlotte snapped her finger in my face. "I swear. Just when I think you are normal, you turn around and go into la-la land. Plus you were just screaming at the top of your lungs. Are you sure you're feeling okay?"

"I'm fine," I assured her.

"I'm not." Mamie Sue gummed and licked her lips. "I told you to find my teeth. Did you? There is no way I can go to a ball game like this." She smacked her lips together. A hollow sound came out.

I giggled.

"I'm fine," I said again to Charlotte Rae. "I'll get the cleaning taken care of before the service tonight if you are *so* busy."

As weird as it sounded, funerals were a big deal

in the South. A big send-off where everyone in town showed up.

In fact, funerals around these parts were bigger than weddings. Women spent hours in the kitchen making food for the after-service. It was sort of a competition to see who made what and whose dish was best. I'd get several calls leading up to the day of a funeral from the Auxiliary women telling me what they were bringing so it wasn't duplicated. I had to keep notes on who was bringing what dish. It was a big no-no to have two of the same food item.

Beulah Paige Bellefry had already called to let me know she had made a new recipe that everyone was going to die for. I was excited to see what it was and how everyone was going to react to it. Especially the Auxiliary women.

The Auxiliary women were a bunch of local women with nothing to do but sit around in their fancy clothes and gossip. Beulah Paige was in charge of them and whom they invited to become a member. One time, they extended me an invitation, but it was quickly recanted after I was diagnosed with the Funeral Trauma.

"Everything is great." I opened the front door of the funeral home and didn't bother saying goodbye to Charlotte Rae before I slammed the door behind me.

Chapter 3

I'm assuming you can still hear me and see me," Mamie yammered.

She continued to keep up with me as I crossed the street. The fastest way to get to the Sleepy Hollow Inn was to cross through the town square, the patch of property in the middle of town that was surrounded by its four major streets.

"Yes." I ducked behind one of the trees and looked around to make sure no one was looking at me. The last headache I needed was someone seeing me talk to myself. Then they'd tell Granny, who would call Doc Clyde, who would then ask me to come in for a crazy check.

I muttered, "This has to be on the down low. I

can't let people see me talking to the air. They all think I'm crazy as it is."

"You aren't!" she protested and stuck her cane in the grass. "You are an angel helping all of us."

"I have a lot of questions to ask you, but first I need to find your file. And Granny will know where that is." I pointed to the Inn.

"Zula Fae?" Mamie Sue asked. She fiddled with the big diamond ring on her finger. "Are you saying that Zula Fae is at the Inn with Ruthie Sue?"

"Granny owns the Inn." I had forgotten that Mamie had been dead before Earl Way had died. I looked around the square to make sure we were still alone.

People were beginning to walk around the square and the streets. Most everything you needed could be found in any one of the shops on one of the four streets that bordered the square. I couldn't let anyone see me, and being sneaky was very important to my Betweener job.

The square was where all the local festivities took place. The parklike setting had a gazebo in the middle, along with benches. Many people spent their lunch hours there, and even the tourists loved to picnic there.

Sleepy Hollow was a number-one destination for cave exploration and hiking the gorges. The mountainous backdrop of our small town was home to many beautiful caves and cave tours. It was our bread and butter for a good economy.

The Sleepy Hollow Inn was on the opposite side of the square. It was as pretty as a postcard, nestled at the foothills of the mountain. Granny owned and operated the Inn after her second husband, Earl Way Payne, died. That was when she retired from the funeral-home business. I wish I could say she left for good, but Granny had her nose in everyone's business. Including mine.

"Earl Way left the Inn to Zula and not Ruthie?" There was an element of surprise on Mamie Sue's face.

"Long story short." I took a deep breath. "Earl Way divorced Ruthie Sue and married Granny. When he died, he left his half of the Inn to Granny. Then Ruthie died"—I left out the part that Ruthie Sue had been murdered and was my first Betweener client—"and Granny got the Inn by default."

"Interesting." Mamie Sue took my explanation without more questions. "I'm sure you don't remember me. I remember you when you were a little squirt running around the funeral home during services. Your momma and daddy used to get on you. But Zula . . ." Mamie Sue shook her head. "She always told them to leave you alone."

I smiled. *The good old days.* The memories were burned in my mind.

"Then I think you went off to school."

"I did." I peeked around the tree. No one was around. "I knew I wanted to follow in my family's business, so I went to mortuary school. What did you do?"

I didn't know a thing about Mamie Sue. Maybe a few questions could lead to answers—of people in her past, along with motives for her murder.

"I did a little of this and that." She shrugged.

The sounds of children caught my attention. They were running and kicking balls with their parents close behind them.

I slipped out from behind the tree and set my sights on the Inn.

The Inn never had vacancies. It was the only place to stay in town, and reservations were made at least a year in advance. Plus Granny's home-cooked meals were to die for. I had tried to talk her into hiring a catering service, but she said there was nothing doing.

"They are guests in my home, and I will cook for them. Good Southern hospitality, Emma Lee." She would shake her fist at me. "That's why Eternal Slumber is so successful. They knew I would take care of their loved ones just like family."

She was right. Charlotte Rae and I did keep things running as smoothly as Granny had. At least most of the time and to the public eye.

The long front porch of the Inn was lined with rocking chairs. They were currently occupied by Inn guests, each with a glass of Granny's sweet tea in hand.

The screen door screeched when I opened it to let myself in. The open foyer was filled with more guests waiting for the dining room to open. They filtered into the room on the right, which Granny made sure to keep stocked with snacks throughout the day.

Running the Inn was right up her alley. She loved to entertain and cook, not to mention how she loved the attention. The snack room was always filled with good cookies, hors d'oeuvres, and tea. Sweet tea.

"Good evening." I greeted Granny with a kiss when I walked into the kitchen. She smelled of cinnamon and sugar. "Something smells good." I stuck my nose in the air and took a deep breath. I opened one of her many stove doors and looked in.

"I guess Zula Fae looks good." Mamie Sue was almost nose-to-nose with Granny, taking a good look at her.

Ahem, I cleared my throat.

"Don't you open that door!" Granny grabbed the towel off her shoulder and smacked me with it. "You are going to ruin my apple pies for Junior Mullins's service tonight."

Granny was such a pretty woman, with her short, flaming-red hair and beautiful emerald eyes. She was a feisty one.

"I have you down for peach pie, not apple pie." My eyes narrowed. I knew I wasn't mistaken. I got excited when she told me she was making my favorite pie. "I think Bea Allen Burns said she was bringing . . ." Realization had set in. Granny was going to sabotage Bea Allen. "Granny!"

"What?" Granny asked, all innocent.

Somehow Granny had known Bea Allen was making apple pie and had changed her dessert. Bea Allen hadn't lived in Sleepy Hollow for years. O'Dell, her brother and owner of Burns Funeral (Eternal Slumbers's direct competitor), ran against Granny for mayor of Sleepy Hollow.

"Bea Allen already signed up to bring apple pie. O'Dell Burns beat you fair and square," I said.

Granny didn't like losing. Especially to a Burns. Our only competition in Sleepy Hollow.

"I didn't know Bea Allen was already in the loop. She did just move back from God knows wherever she has been living. Besides," Granny smoothed her hands down her apron, "she's been gone so long, she's green as a gourd. She doesn't know how to make a good homemade pie," Granny warned, half serious. "Her idea of home-made is grabbing a pie from Artie's."

She picked up the saltshaker and took the lid off the simmering pot of green beans. She shook the hell out of the shaker. Salt poured out. "I don't know why she felt like she needed to move back and run the funeral home for O'Dell. It's not like being mayor of Sleepy Hollow is a full-time job."

Granny ran through the list of mayoral duties. Most of them were just a few minutes here and there, while others were duties requiring a couple hours a week. Still, Granny was right. There was really no reason for O'Dell to lessen his duties as the director of Burns Funeral and let Bea Allen take over.

"And homemade crust?" My eyes widened and my mouth watered.

"She's been working on it all day." Hettie Bell pushed her way through the swinging kitchen doors, shook her head, and put some empty glasses on a round serving tray before filling them with champagne and a chaser of orange juice.

Hettie Bell owned Pose and Relax. It was the yoga studio next to Eternal Slumber. She also worked for Granny when Granny needed her around the Inn. Hettie was good at everything. She cleaned, did laundry, made the guests' rooms look nice, cooked, and even helped Granny serve the meals.

Of course I chipped in when there weren't any funerals to attend to. We all chipped in.

Hettie glanced my way with a little smirk on her face. She blew her bangs out of her eyes. Her face danced along with her smile. She knew Granny was up to something. Granny always was.

"Who told you Bea Allen was making the apple pie?" I asked.

"Mind your own business." Granny shrugged and stirred the green beans before she put the lid back on.

"It is my business. The funeral is my business," I reminded her. "I keep a list of foods and who is bringing what. And you are bringing peach pie." My mouth watered.

"Did you come here to scold me, or did you want something? Because I am busy." She pointed to the door. "I have a line of people I need to feed."

There was no sense in arguing with her. Zula Fae Raines Payne was used to getting her way. Though she lost the mayoral election by two votes, she was bound and determined to come out on top somehow.

If Bea Allen would be mad about Granny's delicious pie, then she was going to have to get mad. It was out of my hands, so I dropped it.

"I'm going to start seating people," Hettie said before she disappeared through the door with the tray of cocktails in her hands.

"Granny, I was wondering about that gravestone with that bell on top of it." I wasn't sure how to bring up questions about Mamie Sue and figure out exactly who she was. Neither Granny nor Mamie Sue seemed fond of the other, but the fact still remained: I needed to get Mamie to the other side. And the only way to do that was to bring her killer to justice.

"I even went to the funeral home and checked the old client files, but there wasn't a file with Mamie Sue's name on it."

"You won't find one. She's a Burns lover." Granny's eyes hooded. "Why do you want to know about old Mamie Sue Preston?" She waved the green bean ladle in the air. Juice went flying everywhere.

"I have never seen a bell on a tombstone like that before." I tried to play it off the best I could. "It's interesting."

Granny took the towel off her shoulder and poured two tall glasses of iced tea. She carried them over to the table and patted the seat.

"Come on over." She took a long drink from one of the glasses. "I need a break. All this talk about Bea Allen and apple pie has got me all worked up."

I sat down next to Granny, but my mind wasn't on drinking tea. I was trying to formulate a way to get into Burns and check out their files, specifically, Mamie Sue's.

"She jumped ship." Granny's eyes peered over the rim of the glass. She took another drink, as if to wash down the nasty taste or thought of Mamie Sue switching funeral-home sides.

According to Granny, you were either on Burns's team or Eternal Slumber's team. If your ancestors were buried at Eternal Slumber, it was the same down the generation. Evidently, Mamie Sue didn't follow in her family footsteps.

"When the old bat died, I went to the family estate to collect the clothes she had picked out to be buried in and found out she had changed her pre-need arrangements a few months before."

Granny's eyes flew open with amusement.

"I'm glad she switched to Burns. She had the ugliest green suit picked out. I mean ugly. I'd rather be buried in a crocus sack than the getup she had picked out." Granny pushed her fingers in her short red hair, giving it a little lift.

Mamie's face drew, her eyes narrowed. She straightened her shoulders, and her face softened. "I want her to know this outfit is made from the finest fabrics. Something you can't get around this town."

"Me," Granny laid her hand on her chest, "I have a gorgeous outfit, so when I see all my men on the other side, they are going to fight over me." Granny winked, stood up and did a little butt shake on her way back over to the counter.

"Good golly, Granny." I laughed. "What am I going to do with you?"

"Love me. Stop asking questions about the dead. Let the dead stay that way. Dead," Granny warned.

"Don't be going and throwing a hissy fit like you always did, Zula." Mamie Sue threw her hands in the air. "It wasn't like you needed my money. You'd been doing just fine on your own."

"I'm curious." I continued to bait Granny. "Please tell me something about her."

"She was in the Auxiliary and everything." Granny slowly nodded her head.

I wasn't sure, but I would bet all the Auxiliary women were Eternal Slumber people, or Granny wouldn't be in the group. There was definitely tension between the two in life, and proving to be in death.

Granny was a grudge holder. She made sure she killed people with kindness and her sweet tea instead of using the cute little pink gun that was in the drawer next to her bed.

"Yep." Mamie folded her arms. "Zula Fae always thought she was large and in charge of the Auxiliary. And I knew she was going to bust a gut when she found out I changed my funeral plans."

The two of them bantered back and forth, neither hearing the other, and making me all sorts of dizzy.

I took a deep breath. Granny rambled on about how evil Mamie was when they were younger, and Mamie spouted back about how Granny thought she was better than everyone else.

I planted my elbows on the table and put my head in my hands. Their voices escalated.

"Enough!" I yelled.

"Well, I'll be." Granny drew back, her Southern accent deep. "How rude of you. You asked."

"I'm sorry." I rubbed my temples. Mamie disappeared. "I have a slight headache, and I didn't come here to get you all upset about someone who is dead. I was asking a simple question about the headstone."

"The bell." Granny's brows extended to the sky.

"Yes. I don't get the bell." I pulled the glass toward me and took a sip of tea.

"I guess they leave the history of the dead out of mortuary school nowadays." Granny tapped the table before she walked over to check the pies in the oven. She pulled one out and put it on the cooling rack on the counter.

"Stop!" I warned Granny when I saw the tip of a cane head straight for her ankles.

"Whoa!" Granny's arms did a windmill. She teetered back and forth.

I jumped up, catching her at the waist before she plummeted to the floor.

"Are you okay?" I got Granny safely on her feet.

"Why," Granny straightened her apron, "I don't know what happened. It was like I tripped over my own feet."

A little cackle filled the empty space around me. I knew it was Mamie Sue hiding out somewhere and watching the show.

Granny looked around the floor.

"I swear I felt something around my ankles." Granny's brow narrowed, then she went about her business.

"Take that, you old bat!" Mamie's voice called out.

"What were you saying about mortuary school and history?" I wasn't going to give any attention to Mamie's bad behavior. "They did go over some history, but what good is history in today's burials?"

Charlotte Rae and I both had to go to school to be undertakers. Charlotte Rae was at the top of the class, as usual, whereas I was in the middle. Regardless, we both graduated, and here we were today.

"Just like Mamie's stone. There are plenty of them out there with bells on them." Granny pretended to ring a bell in the air. "In the old days, way old days, sometimes people were buried alive."

My face contorted.

"They didn't have all the fancy equipment to hear faint heartbeats, so if it wasn't strong, they declared the sick dead." She stuck her tongue out, faking a dead person. Which was in no way how a corpse really looked. "After hearing scratching coming from graves and realizing they were burying people alive, they came up with the bell. The string hung down in the coffin and out to the stone, so if you were buried alive and woke up, you could pull the string. The bell would ding, and they would dig you back up."

"That's terrible."

"How do you think all those people who were buried alive felt?" Granny asked a good question. She walked back over to the table and took a drink.

"And Mamie Sue?" It wasn't like she had died in the time Granny was referring to.

"She was a hypochondriac." Granny sprayed out the tea that was left in her mouth as she laughed out loud. She put her hand over her mouth to stop the stream. "I'm so sorry. But every time I think about how nuts Mamie Sue Preston was, I get tickled."

"I am not nuts!" Mamie appeared. Her face was red, and her hat was sideways. She disappeared again.

"I'm sure she wasn't crazy." I tried to make both of them happy. I had to find some sort of happy medium.

"She thought she had every single disease." Granny nodded. "When AIDS came out in the eighties, she swore she had it. She came to the Auxiliary telling everyone she just knew she had it. Thank God she didn't pass the crazies down. Old Spinster."

"Wait." My mind froze. "She was never married?"

"Married? Virgin 'til the day she died. No siblings. No family. Just her." Granny's words twirled around in my head. "Rich old spinster. Richest woman in Sleepy Hollow, still to this day."

The door of the kitchen swung open. My heart sank to the tips of my toes.

"Ladies." Sheriff Jack Henry Ross stood in the door with his police hat tucked under the pit of his arm.

Our eyes met. His smile widened, exposing his beautiful white teeth. His brown eyes sent chills down my body, making me tingle in places that shouldn't.

"What do we owe the pleasure?" Granny quickly got up and poured my boyfriend a glass of tea.

"I wish I could say it was a social call." He bent over and kissed the top of my head.

I gulped. Had he gotten some information about Mamie Sue Preston before I had told him that she had gotten to me?

I looked up at him. He looked at me. His eyes narrowed as though he was reading my mind. His face softened. He knew something was going on with the Betweener gig. He could read me like a book. He rolled his eyes and shook his head slightly.

"I'm here about a pie and a platter, which is a family heirloom." His eyes slid over to Granny, who had just taken her pie out of the oven. "I got a call from Bea Allen. Someone stole a pie from the kitchen windowsill over at Burns's Funeral residence. It was for Junior's funeral. It's the platter she wants back."

"How terrible," Granny gasped, trying to be all innocent. "Thank goodness I have a pie to take to the funeral."

"What type of pie did you say you had?" Jack Henry asked.

I tried to contain my laughter as he and Granny did a little dance back and forth. Jack Henry would shift to the right to get a peek over Granny's shoulder at the pie on the cooling rack behind her, causing her to shift with him to block the view. He switched to the left, and so did Granny.

"A pie." Granny folded her arms. She wasn't going to admit to anything. Especially if she stole the pie.

"I think Emma Lee keeps pretty good records on who is bringing what dish to the repast." Jack Henry looked over at me for confirmation. I put my attention elsewhere.

Was Jack Henry really trying to get me to side with him against Granny? Was he crazy?

"I can probably get a warrant for those notes if Emma Lee isn't willing to give them up," Jack Henry warned.

"Are you joking me?" I asked.

I couldn't believe he was really taking it to a warrant level. "My hard-earned tax dollars are paying you to investigate a pie?"

Granny clapped her hands and agreed. "Yep. That's right!" She nodded. "Did you say open windowsill? Anything could've gotten her apple pie. A deer. A bird. A possum."

"I didn't say apple pie." A sneaky smile crossed Jack Henry's lips. He knew he had outsmarted Granny. "How did you know it was an apple pie?"

"Jack Henry Ross, when you are as old as I am, you will have gone to as many funerals as me, so you will know people bring the exact same thing each time." Granny was spitting mad. "Emma Lee, fetch me that pot holder."

Granny pointed to the one clear across the room on the counter.

"There's one . . ." I pointed to the one right next to her hand.

"That one." Her face was steady and serious.

"Yes, ma'am." I got up from the table and walked over to get the pot holder. Granny didn't move. She didn't want to let Jack Henry get a look at the perfect apple pie she had just taken out of the oven.

"Heaven to Betsy, y'all get on out of here so I can finish cooking for all of these folks." She shooed us out of the kitchen, putting Jack Henry in a stutter.

"And I just let Zula Fae stop my official police business." He stood outside the kitchen door with a surprised look on his face.

"That's Granny for you." I wrapped my arms around him, curled up on my toes and gave him a good, long, overdue kiss.

Overdue to shut him up.

"Emma Lee, your granny can't go around stealing other people's pies and platters." Jack Henry pulled away.

"You look so cute when you try to pull that cop act." I ran my finger along his strong chin. "Did you forget to shave?"

It was way too early in the day for his facial hair to be sporting a five o'clock shadow.

"I didn't have time to shave because Bea Allen Burns called dispatch, raising all sorts of hell about a robbery. I jumped out of bed and got over there as fast as I could." He pointed to the kitchen. "I know it was just a pie and platter, but it is still considered theft."

"I don't know if she took it or not," I said, even

though I had a pretty good hunch she did. "But I'll look into it. And why would you think Granny did it? Did Bea Allen accuse her?"

"No, Bea Allen was beside herself. She said she put the pie up there at six a.m. and went to get a shower. When she came back out to see if it had cooled down, it was gone." He pulled out his phone and tapped around on it. He held it out for me to see a picture he had taken. "Here is a picture of the crime scene."

"Are you kidding me? Crime scene?" All I could see was the back of Burns Funeral where the residence was located. The window was open, and there was a bush underneath it.

"Look at the bush. Do you see anything?" he asked.

I squinted and shook my head. He used his fingers to enlarge the photo.

"Right there." He pointed to the dirt next to the bush.

There was some sort of tracks. Too small for a car, too big for a bicycle, but perfect for a moped.

"You and I both know only one person in this town with a moped." His lips thinned. "Tell me that this isn't the work of Zula Fae."

"I will look into it," I said and gave him another kiss.

"Ummhmm," he mumbled, knowing good and well there was no way I was going to turn Granny in. "And I can tell by the way you were acting in there that something else is on your mind."

"Nope, nothing is on my mind. Just getting Junior in the ground without a hitch." I brushed off the idea of how he knew I just so happened to be seeing another ghost.

"Nothing. Not even a hint of—"

"Jack Henry Ross, aren't you looking might official," Hettie Bell interrupted at just the right time.

"I'm here on official police business." Jack Henry rocked back and forth on his heels.

"Official?" She seemed amused at how serious Jack Henry was acting.

"I've got to run and make sure the service is still going to run smoothly." I kissed Jack Henry one last time and made a beeline for the door. I mouthed, "Thank you, Hettie Bell."

With a few "good mornin's" I made it out of the Inn and onto the porch, where the rockers were all still occupied. This time, all their bellies were full from Granny's good cooking. I smiled at the group that had gathered. There was nothing like a porch to bring people together. That's the way it was in Sleepy Hollow, and that's what I loved about being from my small town.

I skipped down the front steps and took a sharp right around the Inn. Granny kept her moped chained up to the tree on the side, and I wanted to get a look at the tires.

The tires were spic-and-span clean. If Granny had gone to Burns, wouldn't there be mud or dirt on the tires?

A sudden movement from the window on the side of the Inn caught my attention. Granny was leaning over the counter and looking at me out the window. My mouth dropped. There was a joyful sparkle in her eye.

Right underneath the window was the big plastic garbage can. I marched over and pulled up the lid. Sitting on a nice china platter was a delicious-looking, perfectly browned apple pie with lattice crust.

A shadow drew overtop me. I looked back up, and Granny's face was planted up against the window. Slowly I shook my head and pulled the lid closed.

I had grossly underestimated my granny.

"Take care of this," I mouthed and pointed to the trashcan before I tiptoed back around and across the square back to the funeral home.

Chapter 4

The only clue to a possible motive for someone murdering Mamie Sue was the fact that she was the richest woman in Sleepy Hollow. Money was definitely a motive for murder.

But who? I needed to know more than Granny was willing to tell me about Mamie Sue, and I didn't have the time to figure any more out, but I could make a quick stop over to the *Sleepy Hollow News*, where Fluggie Callahan owed me a favor.

There was some commotion in the viewing room where Junior Mullins was laid out. Charlotte Rae was inside.

"What are you doing?" I asked and looked at the time on my phone.

There were a couple more hours before the funeral was about to start, which gave me plenty of time to make it out to the old mill and put a worm in Fluggie's ear about Mamie Sue Preston.

"After I saw how dusty the curtains were, I noticed how dirty everything else was and started to go through the linens, slipcovers and God knows whatever else is in *that* closet *you* are in charge of." Charlotte's hazel eyes speckled with anger. Her finger jabbed toward the door.

"Pretty is as pretty does," I said, reminding her how her actions were not very becoming of her.

I really wanted to say it wasn't easy solving murders and burying people, but then she'd call Doc Clyde and have me reevaluated for the Funeral Trauma, and there was no trying to explain to her how I saw dead, murdered clients. Though Mamie Sue wasn't a client of Eternal Slumber, she was a Betweener client.

Regardless, it wouldn't sit well with Charlotte. Nor would she believe me.

"Hodgepodge, Emma Lee." She put her hand on her perfectly shaped hip and now shook her slender finger with her pointy pink fingernail at me. "You are in charge of all of this." She twirled the finger around, going right through Mamie Sue's ghost.

Mamie was mocking Charlotte Rae to a tee.

"I'm so glad I didn't have a sister. I would have killed her." Mamie eyeballed Charlotte. "And I'm so glad it's you who can see me, not her. I don't think she'd help anyone."

"I am in charge of this," I confirmed and tried not to bust out laughing as Mamie continued to mock Charlotte.

"I'm telling you. I don't know where Dixie is cleaning now, but she'd do wonders around here." Mamie ran a finger along the chair rail around the room. "It could stand a little dusting."

"If the slipcovers are a little dirty, they should be cleaned." Charlotte pointed her finger to the crown molding along the ceiling. "I can't imagine what that is like up there."

"So what crawled up your butt and died?" I asked.

Charlotte Rae and I were worlds apart, but we had never truly had a knock-down, drag-out fight. And I felt one coming. There was no way I was going to let her talk to me like that.

"I'm tired of losing clients to Burns Funeral." The fury was in her eyes. "I thought we would get a leg up on them when O'Dell took over as mayor, but I was wrong."

"And how is that my fault?" My voice escalated. The anger swelled inside me.

"Take cover!" Mamie yelled over to Junior's dead body. "Emma Lee is about to . . ."

"You are in charge of all the funerals, which includes cleaning! I already spend my days meeting with new pre-need clients, with the accountant, when you are doing God knows what with Granny, who has also gone a little cuckoo lately." She sucked in a deep breath so she could continue her rant. She brushed her hair behind her shoulder and continued, "Plus you are giving big raises out to employees without running it by me first. And while you went across the square to visit Granny, you could've been in here doing your job of making sure this dust was all cleaned! We are going to have so many people in here for Junior's funeral. They are going to judge us not only on how well the funeral is run, but the cleanliness of this place!" Charlotte shouted so loudly that I squinted.

"Call Dixie." Mamie drummed her fingers on Junior's casket. "And please ask her where my teeth are."

"Fine. I'll take care of it," I said, giving in.

Charlotte Rae and Granny might butt heads, but it was because they were a lot alike, even down to the fiery red hair. I could've gone back and forth in a duel with Charlotte and probably won, but it wasn't worth my time.

I had a funeral to host and a murder to solve.

"It's not going to be before Junior's funeral." I cocked a brow. "I have some funeral business to take care of first."

"Then you need to get John Howard in here to dust and make the big raise you gave him count for something." She stormed out, clicking her fancy heels a little louder.

Mamie stuck her cane out right as Charlotte Rae stormed by. Charlotte looked like one of those whirly twirly beanie hats with her arms going around and around. First she teetered on the toe of one foot, and just when she thought she was safe to put the other heel down, Mamie stuck her cane out again. Charlotte Rae tumbled to the ground.

"And that!" she screamed, grabbing her ankle. "Get the carpet guys here to stretch out this old shitty carpet! Or get it replaced with hardwood floors like the rest of this shit hole!"

I choked back laughter and tears.

"Not funny, *Emma Lee*," she said with theatrical bitchiness. "Go find John Howard!" She hobbled down the hall.

John Howard Lloyd was not going to like coming in here to dust. He was great at digging the holes at the cemetery and doing all the landscape work around the funeral home, making sure it was tidy, but he didn't do open caskets.

I waited until I heard Charlotte's office door shut before I went outside to fetch John Howard. He was bent over the flower bed in the side yard between the funeral home and Pose and Relax.

"Hettie Bell told me she loved looking out the window during her yoga classes at the flower bed." He stood up and dusted his dirty hands on the bibs of his overalls. "Says it relaxes her."

"Doesn't he know that's her Southern way of getting him to really keep it looking nice?" Mamie Sue shook her head. "Men always fall for a Southern woman's charm."

I glanced at her, wondering if what Granny said was true. Had Mamie Sue really been a single virgin all her life? And who had her wealth?

"Did she?" I smiled and took note of how much time he had spent on the flower bed. "It looks nice. Now," I clasped my hands in front of me and rocked back and forth on the heels of my shoes, preparing myself for his bemoaning, "I've got some funeral business to take care of before Junior's funeral. I need you to go in the viewing room and dust the crown molding on the ceiling. I think there is one of those long-handled dusters in the closet. Make sure it's good and shiny."

"Didn't y'all put Junior in there already?" he asked with a quiver in his voice.

"Yes, but he's not going to hurt you," I assured him. "He is dead."

"Yes, ma'am, but you know I don't like being around no open casket with them looking at me." John Howard took a step back. "Can't it wait until after I get the closed casket in the ground after the service?"

"You know we have the repast after the service." I turned to walk away. "And I just gave you that big raise too, which means you can have a few more duties. I'll be back to check on your progress."

I didn't wait around to hear what he had to say. It was time to get some answers.

Chapter 5

The old abandoned mill on the outskirts of town was owned by Leotta Hardy and her daughter, Mary Anna Hardy, the owner of Girl's Best Friend Spa.

Not too long ago, the mill was in an unfortunate situation, when it was blown up with me in it. Luckily I escaped, which was another story on a different day, and the bones of the mill remained standing.

Leotta and Mary Anna had come into a little bit of money from Leotta's deceased husband and my former Betweener client, Cephus Hardy. The two women used a little bit of the money to restore the mill.

Fluggie Callahan's old, beat-up, wood-paneled

station wagon was parked in the gravel lot. She said it was all she could afford on a poor man's newspaper salary.

"Looks good in here." I opened the mill door to find Fluggie tucked behind a desk.

Fluggie looked up. Her eyes were magnified behind the glasses perched up on her nose, causing her white eyelashes to jump out even more. Her sandy-blond hair was pulled up in the normal scrunchie-and-bobby-pin look she always seemed to be going for. Her white, short-sleeved collared shirt was tightly tucked into her elastic-waistband capri khakis that were pulled clear up under her armpits.

Her phone rang out a typewriter ring tone. She looked at it and sent whoever it was to voice mail.

"What do I owe this pleasure?" Fluggie asked.

I'd needed Fluggie's help on some information regarding Cephus Hardy, and she'd sort of blackmailed me when she'd found out Granny was running for mayor. The *Sleepy Hollow News* had been shut down after Fluggie had stuck her nose into something someone hadn't wanted exposed, and Fluggie had wanted the paper to be brought back to life even if the Internet was taking over. Needless to say, Granny hadn't won, but O'Dell Burns had been more than happy to bring back the paper. The old mill had been open, and that was where Fluggie had set up shop.

"I need your help and resources." I plopped down in the chair in front of her. "I need some information on a very wealthy woman who was an only child. She's been dead a while, but I'm interested in how much money she had and who she left it to."

"Is this a story I might want in on?" Fluggie asked. "Something you are working on for that little hot number of yours?"

"Story. Maybe. For Jack Henry? No." I bit my lip.

"I likey!" Fluggie banged her hand on the desk. "You know something about this woman, and you aren't telling your man." She scooted to the edge of her seat and planted her forearm on the corner of the desk, leaning in. "I want in."

I shook my head.

"No, no, no," I insisted. "There's nothing to it. No story. Nothing. I just want to know what she did with her money."

Fluggie took the glasses off her face and put the ends of the frame in her mouth. She eased back in the chair.

"Then you can ask around all them Auxiliary women. I'm sure they can give you the gossip. Unless . . ." She took the glasses out of her mouth and pointed them directly at me. "You don't want anyone to know you are snooping around."

My chest heaved up, and then down from a big sigh. Fluggie and I were stuck in a stare down. I needed the information, and she knew it. She had the resources and I didn't, unless I talked to Jack Henry.

"I'm not saying you have to give me any details to why you are looking into this woman's past or financial situation yet." She drummed her fingertips together. "I want the story when you've collected all the data."

"I'm not sure there's even a story."

Of course there was a story. Hell, there was a murder. And I was going to have to make a deal with the devil. Fluggie Callahan.

"There's a story, or you wouldn't have come to me. Just like Cephus Hardy." She clicked her tongue in her mouth. "I haven't figured it out, but somehow you were on to his murder. Was this woman murdered?"

"No." Nervously, I laughed. I couldn't risk anyone finding out how I helped murdered ghosts discover who killed them. "Okay," I went on. I would feed Fluggie just enough to get the information I needed. "I have reason to believe Mamie Sue Preston might have been murdered."

Fluggie grabbed a piece of paper, took the pencil from behind her ear and scribbled away.

"Go on." Her features twisted into a maddening leer.

"She supposedly had millions. But where did they go if she didn't have any family or next of kin?"

"How do you know she didn't have anyone? And where did you come across this . . ." Fluggie put her glasses back on her face and scanned her paper. ". . . Mamie Preston?"

"I noticed her fancy gravestone at the cemetery the other day and I asked my granny about her." I put on my best blank stare so she couldn't read me. "Granny said Mamie was the wealthiest woman in Sleepy Hollow to this day. So that got me thinking. Where is the money?"

"Interesting." Fluggie took the glasses off and tossed them on top of the paper she had scribbled on. "There might be something here. Long shot. But might. It could've gone to various charities."

"Well." I tapped the desk and stood up. "See what you can find out. I'd appreciate it."

Fluggie grabbed her phone, and her fingers flew over the keys like it was a typewriter.

"What are you doing?" I asked, wondering if she was already texting someone to find something out.

"I like to handwrite a lot of things, but I keep all my notes in my phone." She waved her hand in the air. "If one of my contacts calls when I'm not here, I keep notes on my phone so I can add the information. Then I come back to the paper file and write down my new tips or anything I figured out."

"Alrighty, thanks." I walked to the door.

"Tell me, Raines," Fluggie stopped me before I walked out. She had gotten used to calling me by my last name. I took it as a reporter thing. "Are you going through old client files from the funeral home and trying to figure out their lives?"

"Nope. Just a hunch." I left it at that before I disappeared out the door and jumped back in the hearse to head to Junior's funeral.

Chapter 6

When I got back to the funeral home, Mary Anna Hardy was bent over Junior's body. Her big floor lamp was turned on Junior's head like a spotlight.

"What in the world is going on?" I asked and scanned the room. John Howard sat in the front row with his hands folded between his knees.

The smell of Pine-Sol overtook the smell of the fresh flowers that had been delivered and strategically placed around the viewing room earlier in the day.

"Ask him." Mary Anna didn't look up.

She wore tight white pants tapered at the ankle, with black sequined flats on her feet. She had on a bright red wrap top. Her bleach-blond hair was styled in a short bob like her icon, Marilyn Monroe.

"Well?" I walked over to Junior's coffin.

Mary Anna was cutting, hair spraying and combing what was left of Junior's toupee, which wasn't much. The candelabra, positioned at the head of the casket, was a four-tiered candle holder. The candles were usually lit for ambiance during the funeral, but it looked like they had already been burning. There were hardened beads of wax on the holder that hadn't been there earlier. I had made sure new candles had replaced the old ones.

"Miss Emma Lee," John Howard said in a low voice. "I don't like the smell of funeral flowers. They have a certain smell to them. I lit the candles," he admitted. "The lingering smell of death kept creeping up my nose." He used the back of his hand to give his nose a good scratch.

"Not before you put a sheet overtop Junior." Mary Anna didn't miss a beat with the scissors as she told on John Howard. "When he got finished dusting, he whipped off the sheet before he blew out the candles. Junior's toupee went flying right across the flame. The front of his toupee."

Even though Mary Anna had eight stylists at Girl's Best Friend Spa, she also did all the corpses' hair and makeup here at Eternal Slumber. I barely got my own hair done and I rarely wore makeup, so there was no way I was going to be able to do that part of the business. There was no way Charlotte Rae was going to dig her manicured fingers into the hair of a dead person.

Mary Anna said hair was hair and dead or alive, it was all the same. Gave me the groddies but not her.

John Howard looked like he was on time-out.

"Charlotte Rae clouded up and rained all over him." Mary Anna shook her head. "I didn't see all of it. I got her call and came in on the tail end. But I know she gave him a verbal beatin'."

"I'm sorry you had this happen, John Howard." I felt sorry for him. He'd always been a great employee, and I had never had to get on him.

"If you had Dixie this wouldn't have happened." Mamie Sue looked over Junior. "He got teeth in there I can have?"

"Don't worry about Charlotte." I patted John Howard on the shoulder and ignored Mamie. "You can go on. I'll finish up here." I took my phone out of my back pocket and looked at the time.

I had half an hour before this place was going to be filled, and I still needed to get on my regular funeral outfit.

When John Howard walked out of the room, Mary Anna started laughing.

"Charlotte Rae was madder than a wet cat." Mary Anna did another spray of something before she up-righted herself and took a good look at Junior through her bright blue eyes. "I've never seen her so wound tight."

"She's been like that lately. I just ignore her." I looked at the toupee. It wasn't exactly what Junior used to wear, but it was what he was going to wear to his going-away party. "Thanks, Mary Anna."

"No problem." She gathered her things.

"Do you know what happens to a client's false teeth?" I asked, hoping to get some sort of answers that would lead to me finding Mamie Sue's.

"I always leave them in unless their mouths look funny once Vernon sews up the lips." She shrugged. "In that case you keep them out and use filler."

"I want my teeth." Mamie stomped around. "Find my teeth."

"What do you do with them if you use filler?"

"The teeth?" Mary Anna's swooping bangs drew a shadow over her eyes. She tugged the wrap shirt up, covering a bit of her cleavage.

"Yes. The teeth that aren't used."

"I leave them in their file. I guess it's up to you

what you do with their teeth. Maybe give them back to the family or something." She shrugged. "Hell, I don't know."

"Okay. Thanks." I walked out of the viewing room and stopped in the vestibule.

"See you in a little bit." She waved off before she left.

I hurried back to my apartment in the back of the funeral home to get changed.

Charlotte Rae and I grew up in the residence of the funeral home. It wasn't uncommon in the South for a family to own a funeral home and live in it. Same held true for my family. My grandparents lived there with my dad. When my parents married, they moved in and raised Charlotte Rae and me there. Of course it did nothing for my popularity status, which was null because I was known as the creepy funeral-home girl. Sticks and stones . . . right?

Anyway, when Charlotte Rae and I took over from Granny and my parents retired to the sunny state of Florida, we turned the residence into another viewing room off the vestibule and kept a small efficiency for me that included a bedroom, kitchenette, family room, bathroom and small hallway.

I plunked down on my little couch and closed

my eyes. I went over what Granny had told me about Mamie Sue. And over it again. It was too early to know anything, which meant I needed more information.

"Sitting here isn't going to get me my teeth." Mamie appeared next to me. She was busy looking at her ring from an arm's length away. "It's so gorgeous. I love it."

"Yes." I rolled my eyes. "So, do you know how you died?"

"No. But I told Doc Clyde I felt bad. He put me on all sorts of vitamins." She puffed hot air on her ring and polished it on her green skirt.

"Doc Clyde?" That got my attention. "You saw Doc Clyde?"

"Yes. He was the only doctor in town."

"Still is," I grumbled. "He wants to put me in the crazy house."

"Why? Are you nuts and no one told me?" She had an "aw shucks" look on her face.

"No. Before I knew of my little gift." I gestured between me and her.

"Ohhh." She smiled. A look of relief settled on her face.

"I told him I was seeing dead people and he told me I had what was called the Funeral Trauma. Obviously I don't."

"So no one knows about your . . ." Now she gestured between us.

"Jack Henry Ross knows," I confessed.

"And you two are an item?" Her brows wiggled. "I saw you two kissing at the Inn and decided to skedaddle."

"It's nice because he can help. But in your case . . ." I bit my lip. "Your case is a little difficult."

"Why is that? I was murdered just like everyone else that comes to you for help." She huffed.

"Everyone else who has come to me was a client of Eternal Slumber, not Burns Funeral. I can't access their files or try to get their bodies exhumed so easily."

"You are just going to have to try harder." Her chin lifted and she looked away.

"Why did you move your funeral plans?" I asked.

"Zula Fae pissed me off." Her cheek muscles stood out from her narrow face as she clenched her jaw.

"About what?" I asked.

Just like that, Mamie Sue Preston disappeared.

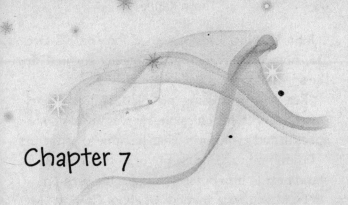

Chapter 7

"Did you talk to your granny?" Jack Henry nodded and smiled as the mourners passed us in the vestibule on the way to Junior Mullins's food line.

The funeral went off without a hitch and the burial just as smooth. No one uttered a word about Junior's toupee. There were a lot of compliments on how nice the funeral home looked. Charlotte Rae beamed.

"About?" I waved to some of the locals and directed them to the room where the food was waiting for them. It was hard to concentrate when the smell of pulled pork, ribs, hush puppies, collard greens, fried green tomatoes, deviled eggs, and macaroni and cheese swirled in the air.

John Howard had a satisfied look on his face. The homemade cooking completely covered up the smell of funeral flowers.

"Bea Allen's missing pie platter." Jack Henry stood tall with his blues on. He was always so respectful and in uniform when he came to a funeral.

I didn't mind, because not only was I proud to stand next to him but it was also a big turn-on.

"I told you, you are way off about Granny." My eyes snapped over to her.

Granny's five-foot-four-inch frame was tucked against the corner of the table, where she was spooning something out of a Crock-Pot onto the plates of Junior's mourners as they passed. She set the spoon down when our eyes met, leaned over and whispered something to Mable Claire, one of the Auxiliary women. Then Granny ran her fingers through her short red hair and looked at me. Her eyes darted to the media room, where the video player for the TVs, controls for the surround sound and anything audio or visual for the funeral home were housed. It was employees only. She ducked into the room.

"You know as well as I know she wasn't making apple pie for this." He looked down at me. His eyes locked on mine. "You told me she was making peach. Your favorite."

"Did I?" I gulped and ran my hand down his arm. "Aren't you hungry?"

There was no getting around Jack Henry when he was on a case. He had great intuition, and I wasn't sure how to shake him. He was like a coon dog on a scent. He wasn't going to stop until he found out what he was hunting for.

"Sheriff. Emma Lee." Doc Clyde walked up and greeted us. "Mighty fine funeral."

Doc Clyde had on his regular pin-striped 1960s suit and his big brown doctor shoes with thick leather soles. He was Granny's latest conquest, and I wasn't sure what she saw in him. And I didn't question it. As long as he kept her busy and out of my business, I was good.

"Emma Lee, have you been feeling okay?" he asked.

Both Doc Clyde and Jack Henry looked at me with a renewed interest.

"I'm fine. Thanks so much for asking," I assured them.

"Wow, he has really aged." Mamie appeared.

"I would like to come in and talk about something," I said to Doc Clyde. I had to get into his office to see Mamie's records.

Jack Henry drew back, his eyes hooded. It was a sure sign he knew I was up to something. I hated to say something to Doc Clyde in front of Jack Henry, but I couldn't shake him.

"Is that right?" Doc Clyde asked with a shocked tone. "Great. Give Ina a call and tell her I said to get you in right away."

"Great. I will." I smiled. "If you'll excuse me. I need to make sure we don't need refills on the food."

I did a quick drive-by around the food tables so Jack Henry wouldn't follow me. I looked back in the vestibule, where he was surrounded by a few citizens. They loved to talk to him to make sure he was keeping Sleepy Hollow safe. When I knew he wasn't looking for me, I slipped into the media room off the viewing room where Granny had disappeared.

"It's about time you get in here," Granny said in a hushed whisper.

"Did you put that platter back in Bea Allen's window?" My brows drew together. "You have done a lot of things, but this takes the cake."

"I didn't do it," Granny protested. "I'm telling you that I didn't do it."

"Oh, ookaay." There was no way I believed that. I poked my finger toward her. "Maybe *you* need a little appointment with your man, Doc Clyde, not me."

"Emma Lee, honest to God." Granny crossed her heart. "I came in the kitchen and there it was."

Granny walked over to a small cabinet where one of the video components was located. She opened the door to reveal the pie plate.

"You brought it here?" I gasped and rushed over, shutting the door in case someone came in and saw it. "What were you thinking?"

"I'm telling you I didn't do it. Someone is framing me, and I'm sure it's Bea Allen herself." Granny's green eyes turned to ice. "I swear," she warned, "I'm going to break bad when I find out."

"Shhooo-we." Mamie Sue cackled. "Someone has got Zula Fae's panties in a wad and thank God it's not me."

Mamie Sue did a little jig around the room. She swung her elbows back and forth while kicking her legs in the air. Her cane was tucked up under her armpit.

"Jack Henry has pictures of the crime scene." I paused to see Granny's reaction.

"Crime scene? Pish posh." Granny waved me off.

"There are tire marks that look just like your moped tires. We both know only one person in this town drives a moped and has a beef with Bea Allen Burns." I pointed to her. "You!"

"Pointing is rude." Granny sighed. "The pie showed up. I knew exactly where it had come from." She shrugged. "Bea Allen is trying to make me look bad, because I bet it was her who put it there." She had it all figured out. "I took the damn pie back and stuck it on the windowsill."

"You did?" I asked.

"I came home and did a couple things for the Inn before I came back into the kitchen and the damn pie was back on the counter." Granny's voice lowered. "I don't know how she got it back there so fast."

For the first time with this whole pie thing, I believed Granny, though I wasn't so convinced it was Bea Allen who was taunting her. These repasts were fierce competition.

"I don't know why, but I believe you." I watched as Granny's shoulders deflated and slumped over. "Now, why on earth would Bea Allen want to say you stole her pie?"

"I don't know. She was at breakfast this morning at the Inn with Jo Francis Ross." Granny's hands flailed about. "And I came back in the kitchen and it was there."

"Jo Francis Ross as in Jack Henry's mom?" I threw my head back.

This couldn't be happening. I ran my hand

through my hair and ended it with a big stretch. Maybe I needed to go to Pose and Relax for a little stress relief. I bounced my shoulders up and down to try to get the knots out of them. The sound of Jo Francis Ross's name made me get an instant headache.

"Yep," Granny quipped. "That's the one."

"She hates me." Sweat gathered on my upper lip just thinking about it.

"How could she hate you?" Granny put her arms around me and squeezed.

"She thinks Jack Henry needs to get a girl outside of Sleepy Hollow so he can become a state trooper and get out of this town." It was a conversation Jack Henry and I had after a few beers at the Watering Hole, a bar on the edge of town, the next county over. I was sure he didn't mean for it to come out of his mouth, because he profusely apologized after he said it.

"And you couldn't be a state trooper's wife?" Granny married me off on my first date with Jack Henry.

"Wife?" I jumped back. "Aren't we putting the cart before the horse?"

"Honey, you ain't getting any younger." Granny made an observation that hurt but was true.

"Anyway," I waved her off. It was hard enough

to admit my first boyfriend was Jack Henry and nearly impossible to swallow how his mother wasn't too fond of me. "Why would Bea Allen want to frame you?"

"I don't know." Granny's eyes narrowed. "You have to find out. In the meantime, you have to get the platter back to her house!"

She pulled her set of keys out of her pocket and dangled them in front of me.

"Me?" I drew back. "Are you kidding?"

"No." She extended her arm closer. "Go on. We don't have all night."

"You want me to leave the funeral to replace the dish? Now?"

"Can you think of a better time? Everyone is here, including the sheriff." She patted a curl here and there.

Granny must've been mad at Jack Henry coming to see her this morning. When she was mad at him, she referred to him as "Sheriff."

"I'm not going to get into why you are mad at Jack Henry. There is no way I can get over there and back without someone noticing." I pushed her keys back. "Plus your tire marks are in the dirt next to the bushes there. You do your own dirty work."

"I thought you said you believed me," she blazed tightly.

"Your face tells me you didn't steal the pie. The hard evidence tells me you did." I held up a finger. "One, the pie was in your garbage. Two," I held up another finger, "you said it was in your kitchen. And three, tire marks."

"I told you exactly what I know. I told you how the marks got there. I'm telling you, someone is out to get me." She closed her mouth when the door opened and Charlotte Rae's face peeked around the door.

"What are you two doing?" she whispered, glancing over her shoulder into the viewing room as she slipped in, shutting the door behind her. "We have a hundred people out there, and you two are in here playing poopsies?"

"Funny." I pushed my way past her and out the door.

Poopsies was a make-believe game our parents used to tell us to go play when they wanted to get rid of us and stop bugging them.

"It's about time someone put Zula Fae in her place." Mamie shuffled past me. I did my best to ignore Mamie, but she let out the most awful shriek. "Dixie!"

Mamie ran off.

Beulah Paige Bellefry and Pastor Brown stood in the doorway between the vestibule and the viewing room. She stood as pretty as a picture with her black skirt and jacket to match, along with a wide-brimmed hat. The lace hung over the hat in front of Beulah's face. Her pearls dripped around her neck and wrist.

She lifted the veil once all eyes were on her.

Pastor Brown was his usual pious self. The sleeves on his brown suit hit his wrists exactly at the too-short line, and his pants hit above the ankle. I wasn't sure why he never bought clothes to fit. His income couldn't be much as the preacher of Sleepy Hollow Baptist Church. There hadn't been any growth in the congregation or any additions to the building, but surely he could afford a suit.

He gave a slight wave when his razor-sharp blue eyes caught mine. I contained my giggle when Mary Anna moseyed over his way and pointed to his hair. She had been dying to get her hands in his coal-black, greasy comb-over.

I kept a close eye on Mamie Sue when she got a little close to Beulah. Beulah's eye swiveled toward Mamie Sue, a dumbfounded look crossed Beulah's face. For a second I thought Beulah felt Mamie Sue next to her.

"Dang. Someone's been to the tanning bed and the plastic surgeon for those lashes." Mamie reached out and touched Beulah Paige's fake lashes.

Beulah waved her hand in front of her face as if to swat a fly; little did she know it was Mamie Sue's finger.

"Dixie?" Mamie's eyes filled with tears. They darted between Beulah Paige and the lady standing behind Beulah, who I only assumed was Dixie. "Are you working for *her*?" Mamie asked Dixie as if Dixie could hear her.

Mamie Sue's face drew from bad to worse. Her nose curled, and she took a big whiff from the casserole-carrying case nestled in the crook of Dixie's elbow.

"Is that my secret chess pie recipe I smell?" Mamie Sue's body stood rigid, her fist clenched. "Oh my God! Dixie!"

"Hello," I greeted them. "I'll take this." I took the carrier from Dixie. "Mmm." I took a nice long whiff. "Is this chess pie?"

"Why yes, it's my secret recipe." Beulah Paige stepped in front of Dixie. "Emma Lee, this is my new maid, Dixie Dunn. Dixie, Emma Lee."

"Her secret recipe my ass!" Mamie took a deep breath and plunged forward, sweeping right through Dixie.

Dixie coughed something fierce. Pastor Brown

put his large hand on Dixie's back and asked her if she was okay. Dixie nodded.

"Let me get you a drink." I had Dixie follow me to the drink table.

Charlotte Rae and Granny had emerged from the media room and were back at their posts behind the serving table.

I handed Granny the chess pie so she could put it with the other desserts.

"Here." I handed Dixie a cup of Granny's sweet tea. "I hope you are okay."

"I have no idea what got into me." Dixie took some sips of tea. "It was like the wind was sucked right out of me."

I stood there getting a good look at Dixie Dunn. She had anthracite eyes and a mop of blond hair. She was definitely younger than I had anticipated Dixie to be. She couldn't have been any more than midforties. She even dressed snappy in her indigo wrap dress, showing off a nice set of gams.

Mamie Sue Preston was what got into you, I wanted to say, only I knew I couldn't.

"Emma Lee." Mamie stepped between me and Dixie. "Don't you dare let anyone eat a bite of my chess pie. Dixie had no right giving my recipe to that, that, that . . ." Mamie turned toward Beulah, who was still in the back of the viewing room where we'd left her. "That hillbilly with money. She stole my pie recipe!" Mamie tugged on the hem of her jacket, gathering her wits.

"So you work for Beulah Paige?" I asked.

"I do," Dixie said between slurps. She handed her cup over the table for one of the Auxiliary women to refill it.

"How long have you been working for Beulah Paige?" I asked, wondering when Beulah Paige got a maid. Even more, when Beulah decided to bake anything, much less chess pie.

"Not long." Dixie's words were short and sweet.

"Woo-hoo, Dixie," Beulah Paige waved a few envelopes in the air.

"Excuse me." Dixie and her tea walked off. "I need to distribute the Auxiliary invitations for her."

"Auxiliary invites?" I put my hand on Dixie. "Is it that time of year again?"

In order to be a member of the Auxiliary Women's Group, you had to be invited by the leader. When Ruthie Sue Payne died, the women voted Beulah Paige as the new gossip queen . . . er . . . president. Another time Granny was knocked out of running for something else.

"I guess." She shrugged and pulled away.

I watched Beulah hand Dixie the invites and utter a few words, which I could only imagine were instructions. Beulah had a funny way of doing things. She called them the proper way; I called it rich people's way of doing things. It didn't seem too proper to be handing them out at a funeral, and that was my opinion.

"I hope you have one of those for me," I said with a big smile on my face when Beulah walked up to get a glass of iced tea.

"Emma Lee," Beulah pulled her lips into a tight smile. "Not this year. I remember you received a generous offer last time and didn't take it."

"I'm going to accept this time," I responded matter-of-factly.

"No." Her smile was still tight to her face. "Not this time."

Dixie walked by, about to hand out her first invite to Hettie Bell.

"You don't want to do that." I patted her arm. "We don't allow solicitations of any sort at funerals. It's not polite." My eyes slid to Beulah. "And Jack Henry is right over there if I need him."

We all turned and looked at Jack Henry. Not his finest moment. His mouth dripped with barbecue sauce from his pulled pork sandwich. He gave a slight wave. I waved back as though he knew what I was doing. It was best to leave him in the dark about my little blackmail scheme.

"Tree!" Beulah pointed to Granny, and then pointed to me. "Apple!"

"What?" For a second, I thought she knew about the apple pie!

"The apple doesn't fall too far from the tree," Beulah spat. Her fists balled.

She grabbed an envelope and handed it to me before she pulled down the black veil and huffed off in a different direction.

"Nice going." Mamie folded her arms next to me. "Now, let's go put that platter back."

Ahem, I cleared my throat.

"I hate to say it, but Zula Fae is right." She lifted her cane in the air. "No one is at Burns, they are here. And that little hot hunk of yours is stuffing his mouth. You aren't on anyone's radar. Beulah wants to stay as far away from you as possible. Plus . . ." Her fine silky eyebrows rose a trifle. "You can look for my file. Grab my teeth."

It only took me a half a second to go back in the media room, grab the platter and dart out the back door.

"You are going to need these." Granny stood on the back porch of the funeral home with her moped keys dangling from her fingers.

In a big toss, Granny threw them at me. I snagged them out of the air and hopped on her moped without even thinking how I had never even ridden the thing.

If Granny could ride, though barely, I could ride it. I didn't bother with the skintight aviator helmet or big goggles Granny wore. I gunned the handle and whizzed down the driveway, turning left before anyone saw me.

Burns Funeral was on the opposite side of town. The hearse would've been faster, but it was blocked in.

Granny and Mamie were right. Burns Funeral was like a ghost town, and it thrilled me to no end to see it that way. I secretly wished it was like that all the time. Thanks to people like Mamie, who switched their pre-needs arrangements without telling us, Burns was going to stay in business.

"Right through there." Mamie Sue pointed to a service door on the side of the funeral home.

The building was really no different from Eternal Slumber. They were both very old Victorian houses turned into funeral homes. The stately brick buildings had wonderfully large rooms with big windows. The crown molding was something new buildings didn't have. The character added to the feel of the importance of a nice send-off. Just like Eternal Slumber, there was a large front porch with a fence. Burns had yellow brick and white trim, Eternal Slumber had red brick with white trim. Both were beautiful, but the employees and owners were quite different.

"Tell me." I put my hand on the door. "Why should I help you when you didn't use Eternal Slumber and you don't like my granny?"

Not that I wasn't going to help her. I wanted her to cross over as much as she wanted to cross over.

"Because I'm paying you." She stood next to me. She was serious.

"Fine." I didn't know why, but somehow I believed her. I would be happy that Mamie would be on the other side to greet Granny if something ever happened to her. And maybe tell Granny about my job as a Betweener, which I felt was far more important than being an undertaker.

"Right there!" Mamie pointed to the large stained-glass window in the only viewing room that Burns had. "I was laid out right under that big, beautiful window."

"Great." I kept going. "Let's hurry."

I had never been in the Burns residence. I had heard it was upstairs and nice. The large staircase stood to your right as soon as you walked in the front door. The Oriental carpet covered each step to the top. Each one creaked with every step I took.

There were two bedrooms. One on the right and one on the left. At the end of the hallway was one big room with a TV, fireplace, and kitchenette.

"Wait." Mamie stopped. "Didn't that hot hunk of yours say it was taken from the window downstairs?"

"Oh!" I snapped my fingers. "Good thinking."

We headed back down the steps and took a swift right turn. The kitchen was much larger for the funeral home, kind of like what we had at Eternal Slumber, but nicer. Way nicer.

There were stainless steel appliances, along with a double oven and gas stovetop.

"Where in the world did Burns get this kind of money to redo this kitchen?" I wondered.

There was a rumor he had done some remodeling to update some things a few years back, but who knew it was this nice. These items cost an arm and a leg now. It must've cost a kidney back then.

My phone chirped a text from my back pocket. My heart jumped. Who figured out I was gone?

Be at the mill tomorrow at nine a.m. It was Fluggie. She must've stuck her nose to the ground and found something out. I stuck my phone back in my pocket and opened the cabinet doors until I found the one with the platters. I stuck the stolen one in and shut the door, closing the who-stole-the-pie-and-platter case.

Too bad the pie wasn't on the platter, or I would have put it back in the window to let Bea Allen think she was going crazy.

"Teeth," Mamie reminded me.

"File." I nodded in agreement.

O'Dell Burns's office was just as nice as his new kitchen. The coffee-colored leather couch was in between Chippendale antique tables flanked by two overstuffed leather chairs and ottomans. The wooden blinds in the window had to be custom made, because when Charlotte Rae and I took over Eternal Slumber, we wanted to get rid of the heavy curtains. When we priced the custom blinds, we decided our clients couldn't see the heavy curtains and kept them. Plus we didn't, don't, have that kind of cash.

"Damn." I looked around. The filing cabinets were built into the wall. "This is costly."

"Yep." Mamie pointed her cane at one specific filing cabinet. "Right there."

I tugged, and it pulled out with ease. I ran my finger along the tabs until I reached Mamie Sue Preston. I pulled it out, and a Ziploc bag fell to the ground.

"Hot damn!" She jumped up, nearly scaring me to the other side. "My teeth! Now, take them to the cemetery and slip them in my hole where the string for the bell is."

"Are you kidding me?" I never really thought about how I was going to get the teeth into her mouth. She was a ghost.

"As long as it's in the casket with me." She pointed to her mouth. Her large diamond sparkled.

"Your diamond ring is in the casket too?" I asked.

She nodded.

"No one in your family wanted it?" I asked.

"Do as I tell you to do. Or you won't be paid." She disappeared in a flash.

"Paid how?" I asked out loud and glanced down at the bag of teeth.

Chapter 8

Junior's repast turned out to be a success, and my little disappearing act to Burns Funeral had apparently gone unnoticed. No one mentioned a word of it. Not even Jack Henry.

After a good night's sleep and another Eternal Slumber client in the grave, I had time for a fresh cup of coffee at Higher Grounds Café before I made an appearance over at Doc Clyde's. Even though he had told me to call Ina, I figured I would show up and insist on an appointment. Ina was already scared of me, and if I threw a little crazy on top of her fear, she would fit me right in the good doc's appointment schedule.

"Good morning," I greeted Ina Claire Nell when I walked up to the counter at Higher

Grounds. "The person I wanted to see on this fine morning."

I was going to have to pull out a good batch of crazy to get on Doc Clyde's appointment schedule this morning.

"Good morning, Emma Lee. How is Zula Fae doing?" Ina's blond frosted hair was piled high on her head. She wore the typical blue hospital scrubs. Only it was scrubs that had to be stolen, because the hospital's name that was stamped all over, albeit faded, was still visible.

Cheryl Lynne Doyle set a steamy cup of coffee and bowl of fruit in front of me. I took the open counter stool next to Ina.

"Granny is fine. Thank you for asking." I picked up the cup and took a sip. "It's me that's not okay."

Slowly I shook my head, opened my eyes wide and stared at her.

"You know." I rolled my finger around my ear like a crazy sign. "I'm all out of meds." I shrugged and popped a grape in my mouth.

Cheryl Lynne laughed. "Ina, your scone will be out of the oven any minute."

Cheryl Lynne walked down the counter, refilling all the regulars' cups before she went over to the cash register to take some to-go orders.

"Doc Clyde said to stop in early this morning to get on the calendar," I said.

Ina's face flushed. She kept her hands around her cup and her eyes forward. The only visible moving part was the lump she was trying to swallow.

"I thought I'd grab me a cup of coffee before I head on over to the good doc's office and hang out until he can see me." I took another sip of coffee.

"He can see you first thing this morning." Ina slapped a single on the counter and got up. "Fifteen minutes."

"Great! I'll be there!" I hollered above the breakfast crowd as she rushed toward the door.

"See you at tomorrow's Auxiliary meeting," a lady sitting next to where Ina was seated called out.

Ina put her hand in the air but didn't look back.

Mable Claire and Beulah Paige passed Ina. They exchanged pleasantries and a few words. Mable and Beulah glanced my way on the way to their normal table.

Auxiliary meeting tomorrow? Seeing how I was a new member, I wondered why they didn't say something last night when I blackmailed my invite from the grips of Beulah Paige.

There was only one way to find out.

"I'm going to move over to that table." I winked at Cheryl and picked my cup up, gesturing over to Beulah and Mable.

"Play nice," Cheryl Lynne warned me when she walked around her counter to go fill others' coffee mugs.

They play nice, I play nice. It was that simple.

"Can I get a to-go cup when you finish with them?" I asked Cheryl Lynne as she passed me. She nodded and made her way through the crowd.

"Ladies." I walked up to Beulah and Mable's table, pulling the extra chair out and plopping right on down. I pulled the folded paper out of my back pocket and put it on the table. I used my finger to un-crease the folds and slid it across the table. "My application for the Auxiliary Women's Group of Sleepy Hollow, and I will pay the fee tomorrow night at the meeting."

"Did you tell her about tomorrow tonight?" Beulah shot a glare at Mable Claire. Beulah's face reddened as deep as her hair.

"Why no, I didn't." Mable Claire stood up and jingled her way toward the bathroom. She ran from confrontation every time.

She stopped when she saw a child. She pulled out some pennies from her pocket, gave them to the child, and patted the child's head before she finally disappeared into the ladies' room.

"I don't know what you have up your sleeve, Emma Lee, but I don't like it one bit." Beulah jabbed her finger on the tabletop. "What is it that you want?"

"I want to be an Auxiliary member." I straightened my shoulders. "Y'all asked last year," I leaned in and whispered, "before I got the Funeral Trauma." I gave a theatrical wink. "All the crazy is gone."

"I'm not so sure about that." Beulah leaned back. She sucked her mouth into the shape of a rosette, followed by a long silence. "I heard you were acting strange in the square yesterday morning behind a tree. *A tree,*" she repeated.

"Was I?" Shit, I wonder who saw me. I had been so careful.

"They said you were talking and talking and peeking and talking." She rotated her hand in the air. "I wasn't going to tell your granny, but I'm not so sure she shouldn't know about it."

"Oh, Beulah Paige, you don't want to do that," I warned and crossed my arms in front of me.

Ahem, Pastor Brown cleared his throat from the next table over.

"Lovely service the other day, Pastor." Southern charm dripped out of Beulah's mouth.

"Thank you." He nodded. He looked at me. "It would be nice to see you at Sunday service, Emma Lee."

"Thank you." I tried to be noncommittal. "Beulah and the girls were kind enough to extend an invitation to join the Auxiliary." I reached my hand across the table and placed it on top of Beulah's. Gently I patted it. She slipped it right on out from underneath and placed her hands in her lap. "Wasn't that nice of Beulah? I'm sure I'm going to fit right on in."

"Mighty nice," Pastor Brown replied. "I hope I see you at this Sunday's service."

He stood up and laid a tip on the table. Cheryl Lynne brought out my cup of to-go coffee. I pulled a five out of my pocket and handed it to her.

"I wouldn't miss service for the world." Beulah was the biggest ass-kisser I had ever seen.

"Now," I drew Beulah's attention back to me. "Where and what time tomorrow night?"

"My house. Seven o'clock." There was a discipline to her voice. "And don't you dare act up, or you won't have another chance. Threats or not."

"See you at seven." The chair shrilled across the tile floor of the café when I pushed back and got up, leaving my to-go cup on the table.

I didn't bother looking back, because I knew

she was spitting mad. Beulah Paige and I had never really seen eye-to-eye. I'm sure it had to do with the fact that I had publicly called her out on her gossip over the past year or so. I did apologize due to the fact I had one too many drinks. Like most Southern women, she didn't forget when someone wronged her. Not even after the apology I had given her.

The only thing I cared about was the invitation to join the Auxiliary. The timing at her house couldn't be more perfect. It would give me a chance to dig deeper into Mamie Sue's past by talking to Dixie Dunn.

If she and Mamie were as tight as Mamie acted, I was sure she had a clue to what happened to Mamie's money. Or at least knew some of Mamie's contacts.

Luckily Doc Clyde's office was in the old house right next to Higher Grounds. Ina Claire had taken her perch on the chair behind the sliding-glass window. She didn't bother opening the window to greet me. She pointed to the clipboard with the attached pen.

Like always, I took the clipboard back to one of the old wooden chairs and sat down. I was careful not to bust one of the cushion ties securely knotted to one of the wooden back spindles. I filled out the form and put it back on the sill for Ina Claire to grab. I still had some time before Doc Clyde came to work, and I needed to get in those files.

The *Southern Living* magazines were piled high between the two chairs. I picked up the one on top. It was dated five years ago. Haphazardly, I thumbed through it, trying to come up with a reason for Ina Claire to move away from her desk. The files were in the pantry right behind her, and no one was going to get past her. Especially me.

"What about Ina's scone?" Mamie tapped the sliding window with her cane.

"What was that?" Ina Claire jumped in her seat. "Did you throw something at the reception window?"

"Me?" I pointed to myself and asked. "No, but I did forget to tell you that Cheryl Lynne told me to tell you that your scone was ready."

It was like giving her a birthday present. The joy flooded right back in her cheeks. The door connecting the hallway of the patient rooms and the waiting room slammed behind her.

"No funny business," she scolded me. "I'll be right back."

"Just going to sit here and read this magazine." I held the century-old magazine up in the air and didn't look up until I heard the outside door shut.

I jumped up and ran over to the door, locking it.

"You are a genius!" I snapped my finger at Mamie Sue. "I wasn't sure how I was going to get rid of her."

I helped myself back to the filing cabinet. Once before I'd had to illegally get a file on my granny, so I already knew the system pretty well. It was alphabetized, and Doc Clyde never got rid of any files.

"What do you want with the files?" Mamie Sue asked.

She peeked over my shoulder when I pulled out the cabinet drawer with the *P.*

"Preston, Preston," I repeated, running my finger down the tabs.

"Are you looking into my file?" Mamie's voice cracked with worry.

"Yes. I need to know what type of illness you really had or even if you did."

"I was always sick. Or at least I had symptoms that Doc Clyde could never diagnose. But my file is none of your business."

"Do you want me to help you or not?" I asked.

"I just don't see how this is helping me."

My finger stopped when it got to *Preston.* I should've known that it was going to be the biggest file in the entire client list.

"Good gravy." I let out a heavy sigh. "How am I ever going to get this thing read before little Miss Receptionist gets here?"

My eyes darted around the office. I wondered where I could put it and get it later.

The handle on the door jiggled. I slammed the cabinet shut and ran back into the waiting room, putting the file on the bottom of the stack of *Southern Living* magazines that were neatly piled on the floor underneath the table.

If the one I was looking at was from five years ago, surely no one would go through the stack on the floor.

"Emma Lee." Doc Clyde seemed to be surprised to see me sitting in the chair. "Is Ina not here?"

"She ran across to Higher Grounds to get her scone Cheryl Lynne made especially for her." I stood up. "You know, I've been feeling really good for the past twenty-four hours. I think I was having a bout of allergies." I sniffed. "I just wanted to pop over and let you know that all is fine."

He stood with his mouth open. The deep wrinkle between his unruly brows creased even more.

"Bye." I gave a slight wave and headed out the door.

I waited a few more seconds before I peeked my head back in. Doc Clyde wasn't in the waiting room. Quickly I tiptoed over to where I had left the file and grabbed it.

"Ina Claire? Is that you?" Doc Clyde yelled from the back.

I tiptoed back over to the door and left.

"Where are you going?" Ina Claire met me on the sidewalk.

"All done. Clean bill of health." I smiled, hugging the file tight to my body.

Ina Claire shrugged and disappeared through the office door. I took my phone out of my back pocket. I was going to be late for my date with Fluggie Callahan.

Chapter 9

I still don't see what my medical file has to do with figuring out who killed me," Mamie cried from the passenger seat of the hearse.

The old mill was past town, deep in the country. The drive was beautiful. The road curved around the countryside and gave a good view of the mountains. It was a beautiful morning. The sun had already chased the morning fog away.

"No stone unturned." I repeated the mantra I had taken to heart since I had become a Betweener.

I had learned I was sort of a ghost private detective. After all, it was me that had to figure out what happened to them. Medical history included.

"You've been dead awhile, and if you don't

have any next of kin for me to question, I've got to start somewhere." I looked over at her. "Plus your headstone reads, 'I told you I was sick.' "

"I know. I laughed so hard when I thought of it." Her face hardened. Her lips puckered around her gums. "I never thought I was going to die from the hands of a murdering sonofabitch!"

"Do you know anyone who had a beef with you?" I asked. "Besides Granny." I eased the hearse around the road and pulled into the gravel drive of the old mill.

Granny and Mamie obviously had a beef, but no one seemed to want to talk about it.

She shook her head. The pillbox hat jiggled. She pulled a couple bobby pins from her hair and used them to keep the hat in place.

My phone rang, and I pulled it out. Caller ID said it was Eternal Slumber. What did Charlotte Rae want now?

"Hello?" I answered.

"Emma Lee, it's John Howard." He announced himself like I didn't know his voice. "Are you coming to work today?"

"I'll be there shortly. I had some business to take care of this morning. Why? Is something wrong?" John Howard never called me. I wasn't even sure he knew how to use a phone.

He came to work every day. Never missed. Once, he was so sick, I made him lie down and sip hot tea. He refused not to work. Hardest working man I had ever seen.

"Nothing wrong. I was just wondering if I could head down and get the sports equipment this morning, since tomorrow night is our first softball game. I wouldn't have time after work to do it and deliver it to the other guys."

"Absolutely!" I hit my head with my palm. I had totally forgotten to tell Jack Henry about the softball league and how I signed him up. "You go on and do what you need to do. We don't have any funerals the rest of the week, so your workload is light."

"Thanks, Emma Lee." John Howard hung up the phone.

Fluggie Callahan was standing in the doorway of the mill, glaring at me. I held up a "one sec" finger and quickly texted Jack Henry.

Eternal Slumber has a new softball team. You are on it. First game tomorrow night. I can't wait to root you on. I put the phone on the seat and got out. Jack Henry wouldn't bother texting back. He would call and ask me why I would put him on the team without asking. This way, if the phone was in the car, I wouldn't hear it ring and feel obligated to answer and then beg him to be on the team.

"Gimme what ya got." I followed Fluggie into her new office space.

Fluggie gestured for me to sit down. She walked around her desk and sat in her chair. She patted her messy up-do and pulled out a pair of glasses. She stuck them on the ridge of her nose and pushed them up.

"Not a whole lot, but I thought you should know she left over a million dollars to Sleepy Hollow Baptist Church." She scanned the insides of a folder before her magnified eyes looked up at me.

"One million dollars?" I asked. "How did you find this out?"

"I've got my informants." She tapped her pencil on the desk. "There is a lawyer from Lexington involved in the entire transaction." She slid a piece of paper across the desk with a name and number scribbled on it. "I smell a rat on this. First off, who leaves a small country church a million dollars? Secondly, I looked into courthouse records about the church, and there haven't been any sort of renovations or anything close to being done that would amount to one million dollars."

I nodded and kept my eye on the paper. There

was a niggling suspicion in my gut telling me Fluggie was right.

"You tell me." She sucked in a deep breath. "What has the preacher done with the money?"

Sleepy Hollow Baptist wasn't the only church in town, but it was the church that all the people I knew attended or at least belonged to. Pastor Brown had to be as old as dirt, and he had been the pastor there for as long as I could remember.

"It isn't unusual for members of the church to leave something to the church in their will." I wanted to debunk any notions swirling around in my head telling me Pastor Brown wasn't as holy as I had always thought he was. "And if I'm not mistaken, I do believe they post those generous donations in the church bulletins."

"Sounds like you need to do some investigating." Fluggie's homely face arranged itself into a grin. "Get your Sunday go to meetin' clothes cleaned and ironed."

"It just so happens I saw Pastor Brown this morning, and he extended a personal invitation to church." I grinned. It was a perfect excuse to nose around.

"I guess I know where you will be tomorrow morning if I need you," she said. "Did you get anything personal on Mamie?" she asked. Her chair creaked when she leaned back, her hands folded in front of her.

"She had a maid, Dixie Dunn, who can't be any older than fifty. Now Dixie works for Beulah Paige Bellefry." I folded the piece of paper and stuck it in my pocket. "I just so happen to be going to an Auxiliary meeting at Beulah's house tomorrow. I want to get Dixie alone, or at least give her a cleaning job at Eternal Slumber so I can question her."

"I've got a few feelers out about where the rest of Mamie Sue Preston's wealth went." She pointed to the blank space between us. "Maybe you can get more information from that lawyer. When I went there, he could smell I was a reporter and called me out on it."

"Undertakers have a way of getting into places." I smiled.

Fluggie and I parted ways with a list of tasks. Both of us agreed to get in touch with the other if we found out something.

My list of questions was growing. The biggest one of all was why she left Pastor Brown the million dollars and why there hadn't been any gossip about it.

That was the type of gossip that would have spread like melted butter on a piece of toast, but

Pastor Brown had never mentioned a word. Not even to the congregation.

It looked like I'd be taking a spot in the front pew of Sleepy Hollow Baptist tomorrow.

The roar of absolute silence hung between me and my ghost friend on our way back into town.

"Sooooo," I dragged out the word for more emphasis, "do you want to tell me why you left Sleepy Hollow Baptist one million dollars?"

"It's the right thing to do." Her words were short and direct.

"What does that mean?" I asked. "Feed the needy. Feed the animals in the animal shelters. That would be the right thing to do."

"It was my money, and I got to decide what I wanted to do with it. Just like I wanted O'Dell Burns to bury me!" Mamie pounded her tiny tight fist on the dash of the hearse.

"And I'm the Betweener who needs the answers to these questions so I can help you get to the other side!" I yelled back, which didn't prove to solve anything.

Mamie Sue Preston disappeared into thin air.

She was protecting someone, and I was going to find out who. Unfortunately, the person might be her killer.

Chapter 10

If Mamie wasn't going to help me out with simple questions, I wanted to just forget about helping her, but she and I both knew *that* wasn't going to happen. I was going to have to figure this out without her help, and I didn't care who she was protecting. Even if it was a man of the cloth.

The Sleepy Hollow Courthouse held as many secrets as the Auxiliary women. If you knew exactly where to dig, the answers would show.

I pulled the hearse into the parking space right in front of the oldest structure in town. The three large concrete pillars held up the ornate design. Several large steps led up to the heavy lead-glass doors. The marble hallways echoed with each step as I made my way to the records room.

"How can I help you today?" The deputy clerk looked up from her filing cabinet and swept her bangs to the side.

"I think I've got it." I smiled and helped myself to the public files in the back of the room.

Things such as deeds, marriage certificates, wills, taxes, anything public was located there. Anything public on Mamie Sue would be there. Including her street address.

Addresses was more like it.

Mamie Sue Preston held the deed to not only a mansion in Triple Thorn, the wealthiest neighborhood in Sleepy Hollow, but also the building where Pose and Relax was located, as well as the deed to Sleepy Hollow Baptist Church along with a house in the country. The properties were left in trust with Emmitt Moss, Attorney at Law, as trustee of the DD LLC. The land deeds showed the properties changing from Mamie to the trust as well. Who did the trust go to? Who was this lawyer covering for? And who or what was DD LLC?

Is Emmitt Moss the lawyer you went to see? He is the trustee for the trust for DD LLC. Mamie owns a bunch of property, including Sleepy Hollow Baptist Church. All the property went to a trust at DD LLC. I texted Fluggie. She was good at looking into those types of things, and I was good at sniffing out people.

I used the notes section on my phone to type in the Triple Thorn address, which I plugged into my maps. It was time I went to see some neighbors about sweet little ole Mamie Sue or poke around to see if anyone had a need for pre-need funeral arrangements.

The mansions in Triple Thorn only reiterated I was in the wrong business. There wasn't hardly any money to be made after a funeral and Charlotte Rae took her salary. We had agreed she'd make more money, since I was living at the funeral home and using all the utilities I needed. There was something to be said for dead people. Job security.

Still, these houses were colossal. All of them had at least five or six roofs peaking at all different pitches. Not to mention funny-shaped trees. Some lawns had tree animals, while others had water fountains big enough for me to swim in.

I pulled the hearse into Mamie Sue's driveway and stopped right at the privacy gate. I got out. With my hands on my hips, I looked around me. There was no getting in there unless I hit the button. I wasn't sure if anyone was there, but I did know DD LLC was the owner.

"Hello?" I pushed the button several times.

"You can stop hitting the button. One time is

sufficient," a woman's voice answered through the speaker. "No one is dead here."

"What?" I asked, my finger still holding the button down.

"Stop holding the button. You can just talk," the woman instructed me. "The hearse. No one is dead."

"Oh. You can see me?" I asked, looking around for a camera.

"What do you want?" she asked again.

"I had a few questions about the owner of the house, Mamie Sue."

Dead silence.

I leaned into the box. "Hello?"

"I'm here." She paused. "Okay."

Buzz, buzz. The gate started to move. I jumped in the hearse and drove up the long blacktop driveway. The landscapers stood up on those fancy mowers and zipped around the trees and wrought-iron fencing. There were a couple of guys hand-trimming the edging with scissors. I didn't envy their job. My back hurt looking at them.

Mamie Sue had definitely known how to live. Her white colonial home had a fenced wrap-around porch. The outdoor furniture looked like it cost more than what I would pay for indoor furniture. I could definitely get lost in one of the large comfy cushions.

I got out of the hearse.

A stick-thin young woman with an apron tied around her stood at the top of the colonial steps, her hands clasped in front of her.

"Can I help you?" she asked in the same voice from the call box, only very low now, almost whispered.

"I wanted to talk to the person who lives here now," I informed her.

"They aren't here." She didn't budge from her post in the middle of the steps. "What did you want to know about Ms. Preston?"

I had to lean a little closer to hear her.

She wasn't messing around. Her hair was a plume of black in a low ponytail at the nape of her neck. There was no way she was much older than me. Thirties at the oldest.

"Can you tell me who owns the house now?" I asked.

"Ms. Preston still owns the home." She wasn't offering up much information or expanding on my question. She peeled off a long, heavy-duty yellow cleaning glove. "I just clean here."

"I thought you said the owner wasn't here at the moment, so if Ms. Preston owns it still—"

She interrupted me. "You asked me if the person living here was here. They are not here. Now, I have to get back to work."

"Can you please tell the *person* living here to give me a call?"

"I suppose."

I rushed back to the hearse, grabbed an Eternal Slumber brochure from the glove box and ran it back up the stairs to her. There was a familiarity to her eyes.

"Did you go to Sleepy Hollow High?" I asked.

She tugged on the brochure until I let go. "No." She turned and walked back into the house. The sound of dead bolts sliding into place on the other side of the door was followed by the sound of footsteps walking away.

My mind was lost in what had just happened. The girl looked familiar, and I was having a hard time figuring out what it was that had resonated with me. One thing I did know, someone involved with DD LLC lived there, but who?

I pulled over in the next driveway down and sat, trying to recall everything the conversation had held.

Fine. I'll be on the team, but you have to have dinner with me and my parents tonight at their house. My phone chirped a text from Jack Henry.

Blackmail? I texted back.

Only if you are going to continue to be my girlfriend. He texted back a response I wasn't going to fight.

His mom's words the last time I met her played in my head. *"So what are you going to do with your life, Emma Lee?"*

He must've read my mind. He texted, *Stop thinking my mom doesn't like you. I love you! I'll pick you up at 5.*

I texted back a heart emoji, which he hated. He said emojis weren't a form of communication and when did they become punctuation. Just for spite, I sent a smiley face as well.

A car pulling up to Mamie's gate got my attention. It was a long blue station wagon with a sign on the side that read DUSTING DIXIES and included a dancing feather duster image.

Someone was still paying for a cleaning service and the landscapers, plus the woman who answered the door was dressed as a maid. Who was funding this? There wasn't an estate.

I had a couple hours until I was going to meet Jack Henry at the funeral home. I ran through the McDonald's and got me a large Diet Coke with extra ice. I needed the extra caffeine if I was going to have to deal with both Jo Francis Ross and a fancy Lexington lawyer.

Chapter 11

MOSS AND SON, ATTORNEY AT LAW was scrolled in gold lettering on the glass door. The reception area was really nice. There were leather chairs, and only one was occupied.

"Hi." The receptionist smiled. In a chirpy voice she asked, "How can I help you?"

"I'm with Eternal . . . um . . . Burns Funeral in Sleepy Hollow, Kentucky. I need to talk to Emmitt Moss about a client of ours. Mamie Sue Preston." I didn't feel one bit bad for lying.

Mamie Sue might be hiding something from me, and it might not have to do with her murder, but now my curiosity was up. Which was not a good thing. A Southern woman always wanted to be seen as a lady, but really, we were all nosy.

The receptionist held a finger in the air and jumped out of her seat.

"Hold on," she quipped. A wary, haunted look crossed her eyes before she rushed down the hall and into a room.

A few seconds later she and a stocky older man in a black suit with a nicely manicured goatee emerged from the room.

He looked at me, said a couple words in the woman's ear and gestured for me to come on back.

"Thank you for seeing me without an appointment, Mr. Moss." I held my hand out. "It seems that I had never gotten a final payment from Ms. Preston's estate regarding that special bell stone of hers."

"Years have passed. This matter should have been taken care of a long time ago." His brows hooded his curious eyes.

"I know. It was an oversight on our part. I'm not sure if you are aware, my brother, O'Dell, was elected mayor of Sleepy Hollow, and I have taken over." I smiled, gave a little wink and deepened my accent. "Of course I'm learning the business side and going through the books. Unfortunately, Ms. Preston wasn't the only one O'Dell let slip through the cracks."

He sat in his chair and leaned back. He put

his hand on his chin, giving his goatee a good scratch.

"I know you are a busy, busy man and I hate to bug you with this." I planted my hands on his desk and leaned way over. "I'd be more than happy to contact them myself if you want to give me the contact information to DD LLC."

His eyes had a hard time focusing on my face. I had never used my body to get what I wanted, but there was a first for everything.

Ahem, he cleared his throat. His eyes looked at me. I dragged myself off the top of the desk.

"Miss . . ." He searched for my name.

" . . . Burns." I reminded him of whom I was pretending to be.

"Burns. Miss Burns." He said it like he was trying to remember it. "Sally will get the contact information for you if you would like to leave your number with her." He stood up and adjusted his pants. "Or we could just skip that step and you could give it to me." A sly smile crossed his lips, exposing a gold eyetooth.

"Thank you." I waved and headed out the door.

There was no way I was going to give a slime-ball like him my phone number. I guess my assets didn't work the way I wanted them to.

"Aren't you going to give me your number?"

Sally the receptionist asked as I walked by and out the door.

I took a long sip of Diet Coke once I got back into the hearse. There was something fishy going on with all this. There were too many hands in Mamie Sue's financial pot, but who was the killer? I had an eerie feeling the killer was someone I had already met. But which one?

I looked at my notes on my phone to see if anything at all would click. Wealthiest woman in town. Dixie Dunn, Emmitt Smith, Pastor Brown, million-dollar donation to the Baptists—where was it? And Mamie owned the building for Pose and Relax.

"Pose and Relax." I smacked my hands together. "Namaste."

I turned the hearse back toward Sleepy Hollow. It was time to get my Zen on. Hettie Bell rented the building. And if the building was in Mamie Sue's estate just like the courthouse documents stated, Hettie Bell had to know who was cashing her checks.

It didn't look like Charlotte Rae had bothered coming to work. Her car wasn't in the back parking lot of Eternal Slumber when I pulled in and parked. I quickly changed into the only pair of yoga pants I had and walked next door to Pose and Relax.

I was happy to see Hettie Bell through the window . . . alone.

"Hey!" There was an element of surprise in her face when I walked into the studio. She looked like a fit yoga girl in her black yoga pants with pink stripe up the side. She had a T-back tight yoga shirt to match the pink on her pants. She turned around to straighten the brochures on the counter; YOGA GIRL was printed on her butt in pink. "What are you doing here?"

"You've been begging me to try all this crap. I mean Zen." I sucked in a big deep breath. "So have your way with me."

Her lips pursed suspiciously. "Cut the bull. What do you really want?"

"Damn. I thought the yoga pants were a good cover-up too." I smacked my legs. "How did you hear about this place to rent?"

"Why do you ask?" Hettie asked. She leaned on the glass counter and folded her arms. "Usually when you start asking weird questions, something is up your sleeve. Kind of like the time you took me to the Watering Hole."

"I'm trying to figure out the history of the building and who owns it. Granny had mentioned my grandfather was going to buy it." I shrugged. "It got me curious."

I walked over to the middle of the yoga floor. I threw my hands in the air and plunged myself forward into some sort of pose I made up on the spot.

The board under me creaked. I scooted my foot an inch and it creaked more.

"Curious enough to pretend to want to do yoga?" Hettie Bell was maybe a couple years younger than me. She wasn't stupid and was proving to be a good businesswoman. "I've got to get that board fixed. It just started creaking, and there's nothing less Zen than a creaking board."

"Just tell me and I'll get you a beer from the Watering Hole with no strings attached." I cut to the chase. A big grin spread across my face and I lifted my brows, along with my shoulders.

"Hold on." She sighed and walked through a door that had a black plate with OFFICE engraved on it.

My phone chirped from the waistband of my yoga pants.

DD LLC = Dusting Dixies owned by Dixie Dunn, Fluggie texted.

The maid???? I texted back.

Yep. Still digging.

"Dixie Dunn?" I asked out loud. "Did Mamie Sue leave her wealth to her maid?" I asked in a hushed whisper when I heard Hettie shuffle back in the room.

"I had gotten the listing online at craigslist and emailed this lawyer." She handed me the paperwork she had printed off the computer.

"Emmitt Moss." I read the name and noticed that the P.O. box's zip code was Sleepy Hollow's one and only zip code. "DBA, DD LLC." I looked up at Hettie. "Say, can I get a copy of this?"

"Sure." She wiggled the paper out of my hand. "I'll be right back."

A couple of people with yoga mats came in. They laid their mats on the hardwood floor in front of the large mirrored wall and started to stretch. The big chalkboard on the wall had the list of daily classes. There was a stress relief class starting at four thirty, which meant I only had thirty minutes to get all gussied up for my dinner date with Jack Henry at his parents' house.

It really didn't matter how much time I had. Her Royal Highness Kate Middleton could be his girlfriend and Jo Francis Ross still wouldn't approve.

"Good afternoon, ladies," Hettie greeted the yoginis and handed me the paper. "Class will start in a few minutes. You probably want to move up. I have a creaky board there."

The girls rocked their bodies back and forth to find the board.

"Nothing. See." Hettie threw her hands in the air. "Damn board has a mind of its own."

"Breathe in Jesus, breathe out peace," I said and laughed.

She closed her eyes and pretended to breathe. She laughed.

"Have you met Emmitt Moss?" I asked.

"No." She shook her head. "I have to mail the payment to the P.O. box by the first of the month. Which reminds me . . ." She bit her lip. "That's tomorrow. I'm going to have to have the postal worker stick it in the box." She winked. "He's a cute single guy that doesn't mind doing me a favor now and then."

"I bet." I held the piece of paper up in the air and thanked her before I walked back over to Eternal Slumber.

My tomorrow was quickly filling up. First church, softball game, and the Auxiliary meeting. It looked like stalking the post office was next on the list.

I wondered who I was going to see. Dixie Dunn or Emmitt Moss.

Chapter 12

"Wow!" Jack Henry stood on the doorstep of the residence entrance of Eternal Slumber. He had a cute boyish look on his face. "You look *great*."

"Let's hope Cruella De Vil likes it." I couldn't help the rude comment.

I had opted to wear a pair of skinny khaki pants, tight black sweater, and a pair of black flats, attempting my best to imitate Audrey Hepburn's infamous look.

"Okay little Zula with the snide comments." He pressed his lips together. His jaw tightened.

"I'm kidding. Thank you. You look nice too." I noticed how cute he looked in his collared shirt, khaki pants and loafers.

He wrapped his arms around me, and with his hand on the small of my back, he pulled me in for a kiss. Thank God he was holding me, or I would have fallen on the ground from the weakness in my knees from his soft lips.

"Or we could skip dinner and head into the bedroom for dessert." I did my best to persuade him into not going.

"Then you'd really give her a valid reason not to love you." His mouth moved down my chin and found my earlobe. He nibbled. "And I want her to love you as much as I love you."

I guess there was something cute about the way he loved his mom. Only I didn't see what made her that way in his eyes. She always seemed to be on his ass about getting a better job, better life, better girlfriend.

"Fine." I pushed off. "If we keep doing this, I'll never care if she likes me or not."

"Love. Love you," he repeated.

"That," I jabbed my finger in his chest, "will never happen."

"We'll see." He grabbed my hand.

On the way out I grabbed the little black cocktail purse I'd snagged from the client closet. It was a closet where we put the extra clothes loved ones sent in for their family member to be buried in.

Most times they would send us a couple of different outfits. When we would try to give the extra set back, they said to keep it or donate it to a family that needed funeral clothes.

Lucky for me, the little bag was perfect to keep my phone in just in case I heard from Fluggie.

"Tell me about this softball league you've gotten me into." Jack Henry pointed to the back seat of his cruiser. "John Howard brought my uniform to the station today."

"Grave Diggers?" I read the T-shirt and laughed. "Eternal Slumber's softball team is named Grave Diggers?"

"He was so proud of it." Jack Henry turned the cruiser past the square toward the old mill.

Jack Henry's parents' house was out that way. Since we had started dating, I'd only been invited out there a couple times.

"I really don't know much about it." I pulled the visor down to help block the sun from my eyes. "He came in the office hemming and hawing around. He mentioned Burns, so I figured he wanted a raise." I reached over and put my hand on Jack Henry's leg. It was still a dream come true for me to be dating Jack Henry Ross. "I gave him a big raise and tried to send him on his way, but he kept on. And I gave him another raise." I started to laugh. "John Howard got two raises within minutes. Charlotte Rae about died. Anyway, he really wanted to ask me if the funeral home would sponsor the team."

"So you volunteered me?" He kept one hand on the wheel and rested the other on top of mine.

"I'm dating Sleepy Hollow High's best baseball player ever." I leaned over and kissed his cheek. "You are my secret weapon against Burns."

"You're using me." He laughed.

"In more ways than one." I kissed his neck.

He eased the cruiser to the side of the old country road and put it in park.

He put both hands on my face and pulled me into his arms, his lips sending shivers of desires through me.

"You're going to drive me crazy all night until we can get back to your place," he whispered into my hair.

He put his hands through my long brown hair. Stopping at my neck, he drew me closer. This time his kiss had a passionate message that was received. I felt like the girl I wanted to be in high school. Every single night before I went to bed, I dreamed of Jack Henry kissing me just like this.

"We better go." I put my fingers up to his lips. "Before we really are late."

He released me and let out a deep sigh.

"Woowee, you drive me crazy, Emma Lee Raines." He ran a finger down the side of my face before he put the car in gear and peeled out.

I had to take several deep breaths to get my breathing back to normal.

"I did want to tell you that Bea Allen Burns called me today." He gripped the wheel to make the turn into his parents' driveway. "She said the platter mysteriously appeared in the cabinet of the funeral home. Clean and everything."

"Hmm." I moaned.

"I'm guessing you are going to deny knowing anything about that?" He put the car in park.

Bolt and Rocky, the family's two big black Labrador retrievers, bounded toward the car at full speed.

"Not a thing." I stepped out of the car.

If Jo Francis didn't like this outfit, it was only because she really did hate me.

"Down boys," Jack Henry coaxed the rambunctious pups.

They didn't listen. They hopped and jumped, hoping to get the attention of Jack Henry's hand that was helping me out of the car.

"Oh, I'll love on you." I bent down, getting smothered in wet doggie kisses.

"Jack Henry, I hope you don't kiss that mouth." Jo Francis's voice rang in my ear like a lightning bolt and pierced my heart.

"He kisses more than that," I uttered under my breath, stood up and smiled.

"Mom." Jack Henry's displeasure was apparent. "You know you let them kiss all over you too."

Jo Francis had on the latest trends. She was the cool mom when we were growing up. Cool as in had the svelte mom body with the clothes to match.

She had on a pair of skinny cropped jeans, boat shoes, light blue sweater and a large silver beaded necklace. Jack Henry got his dark brown hair from her. Only hers wasn't cut high and tight like his. Hers cascaded down her shoulders. Long and straight, full body.

"Did you get highlights?" she asked. Her eyes drew up and down my body, getting a good drink.

I raised my hands to my head. My black clutch dropped on the ground. Bolt grabbed it and ran off as fast as he could.

"Damn!" I screamed and took off after him.

"Yes, I hope you don't kiss that mouth." Disgust dripped from her lips

I didn't bother looking back; I did a leap in the air, hoping to nab Bolt before he leapt into the pond. It was too late. Both of us ended up in the knee-deep water, covered in moss and muck.

"Are you okay?" Jack Henry stopped at the edge of the pond. "Bad dog!" he scolded Bolt.

Bolt dropped the purse in the pond and took off in the other direction.

"Come on, let me help you out." Jack Henry put his hand out.

"Damn dog." I grabbed my purse and opened it. Water and a dead cell phone fell out into my palm.

"I'll get you a new phone." Jack Henry's eyes grew openly amused.

"Stop it." Tears burned at the edges of my eyes. I sludged through the muck. "I want to go home."

"No. I have clothes here." He grabbed me by the elbow.

Out of nowhere, Jo Francis was next to us with a big towel. Jack Henry took it and wrapped it around me, leading me up to the house.

"I am sorry about Bolt. I have no idea what got into him," Jo Francis said.

Only I didn't believe her. She probably taught the dog the trick before I got there.

"You can go into the guest room to get a shower. I'll get you a towel." She tried to take the lead.

"No, Mom." Jack Henry pushed her hand away.

"I'll take her to my old room and she can shower in there."

"But . . ." Jo Francis tried to protest.

She quickly shut her mouth when Jack Henry gave her the death stare.

The house smelled of pork roast, potatoes, and fresh garden green beans. They had a one-story ranch home with an attic converted to a suite for Jack Henry. There were three bedrooms and four baths on the one level. Jo Francis had used an interior decorator in the traditionally designed house. Most of the patterns were deep red plaids and horse items. The entire house had hardwood floors with deep mahogany crown molding. The hardwood was flanked with Persian rugs that had been imported from overseas.

Jack Henry had grown up in a luxurious life that horses and tobacco farming offered. The dead and burying the dead were not comparable.

"Thank you," I said when Jack Henry shut his bedroom door behind us.

He gripped the edges of the towel and pulled me to him.

"I love you." He kissed the tip of my nose. "You are right. I need to set Mom straight. She's going to lose me if she doesn't come around."

"She thinks I'm nuts and not good enough for you." The tears kept coming.

He took the edges of the towel and dabbed at my eyes. His face softened into a warming smile.

"You aren't nuts, and you are too good for me." He turned me to the bathroom. "Go get a hot shower, and I'll put a T-shirt and sweatpants out for you from my drawer."

I did exactly what he told me. My heart was warm from his words. It was what I needed to hear to get through this night. I peeled the nasty pond-water clothes off my body and looked in the mirror. I knew better than to try to apply makeup, when I rarely wore it. The mascara was thick and black under my eyes, and it streaked down my face, not on the eyelashes, where it was supposed to stay. So much for waterproof.

The showerhead was one of those with multiple streams. I closed my eyes and let the hot water roll over me. The idea of being in Jack Henry's shower filled me with love, but it wasn't enough for me to forget about my phone. All the notes I had been putting in there about Mamie Sue Preston were now lost. When I got home, I was going to have to sit down and write them down while they were still fresh in my mind.

I heard voices coming from the hallway when

I stepped out of the shower. Jack Henry and his mom were outside his room in a heated argument.

I snugged the bath towel around my body and tiptoed to the shut door, putting my ear to it.

"I'm telling you, something isn't right with her," Jo Francis warned her son on the other side.

"Mom, I love her. You are going to have to accept that."

I smiled, closed my eyes and took a deep breath.

"Bea Allen told me Emma Lee pretended to be her today at some lawyer's office in Lexington."

My eyes shot open. *Shit, shit, shit!* So much for keeping Mamie Sue a secret from Jack Henry.

"What are you talking about?" Jack Henry sounded confused.

"Bea Allen called and asked if you were still dating Emma." She let out a heavy sigh. "Then she told me Emma Lee is asking all sorts of questions about one of their customers." She hesitated. "Mamie Sue Preston. Emma tracked down Mamie Sue's lawyer and drove to Lexington to see him. She lied, Jack, honey. She told the lawyer she was Bea Allen and that Mamie Sue's estate owed her money."

"This doesn't make sense. I'm sure there is an explanation," he reasoned.

First, I didn't say I was Bea Allen. I said I was

with Burns. I maybe alluded to it, but I didn't say Bea Allen.

"Then Bea Allen told me that her platter was missing and she told you about it. You did nothing about it because it was Emma's crazy grandmother who stole it." Her voice held anger. "I'm telling you, you are going to lose that job offer if you don't get rid of her."

Job offer? My ears perked up.

"I'm not getting rid of her. And besides," he hesitated, "I'm not sure I want to take the job and move away."

"You get your head straight, young man," Jo Francis warned her only child. "You've worked all your life to get a good education. Think with that brain of yours, not your penis."

I rushed back to the bathroom and quietly shut the door when I heard Jo Francis's footsteps walk down the hall.

I sat on the toilet seat. There was an old Sleepy Hollow High baseball T-shirt and sweatpants on the sink counter, nicely folded.

I bit my lip to stop me from crying. It seemed Jack Henry and I were both holding secrets from each other. It was obvious he had been offered a state police job that required him to move away and I was the one keeping him from fulfilling his lifelong dream of moving up in a job he loved so much.

"Are you out?" Jack Henry tapped on the door. "I put some clothes that should fit you on the sink."

"I saw them. Thanks." I gulped back the tears.

I pulled the clothes on and opened the door.

"Do you have a hairbrush?" I asked. My heart felt like it was being torn right out of my body when I looked at him, knowing he was hanging his dreams out to dry.

"Yeah," he said and disappeared.

I sat on the edge of his old bed. It was time I let him off the hook about the job. I would tell him we could do the long-distance thing and encourage him to take the job.

It wasn't like Kentucky was such a big state that we couldn't.

"Here you go." He sat down next to me and handed me the brush. "If I'd known you looked so damn sexy in my high school shirt, I would've let you have it in high school." He drew back when he noticed I didn't respond. His brows furrowed. "What's wrong?"

"I . . . I overheard your conversation with your mom."

"You have to ignore her. I'm sure there was a

mix-up about Bea Allen." He rubbed his hand down my spine and scratched the small of my back. "You didn't do that, did you?"

My body tensed.

"Emma Lee, did you?" He removed his hand. His big brown eyes popped open. He knew. He stood up and ran his hands through his hair. "Good God, Emma. What the hell? I'm a cop. Impersonating someone is a felony."

"I needed to know some information about Mamie Sue Preston." I prepared myself for what was coming next.

"Who?" He shook his head. Disappointment lay deep on his face.

"Mamie Sue Preston," I whispered and looked down at my hands. I picked at my fingernails. "She was murdered."

Chapter 13

I figured out the quickest way to get rid of Jo Francis Ross. Tell Jack Henry someone was murdered.

"How long have you been helping her?" Jack Henry's jaw muscles were as tight as his fingers gripping the steering wheel.

"A few days." I didn't look at him.

I kept my focus out the window. The trees and background were blurred; Jack Henry was going fast.

"Please slow down," I suggested.

"I truly can't believe you have been investigating a murder on your own." He beat the wheel with the palm of his hand. "Do you know how dangerous this is? You could cross the wrong person and they wouldn't have any problem killing you. Then what would I do?"

"You would take the big job you were offered that you didn't tell me about."

The silence in the car made my arm hairs stand on end.

"You didn't think I heard that part?" I asked. Anger began to swell in me. "And that your mom thinks I'm holding you back from your lifelong dream of being a state trooper? How could you keep this from me?" It was like he opened up a can of worms, because I couldn't stop my mouth. "Talk about feeling stupid. You are my boyfriend! This is a big opportunity for you. How do you expect me to be able to accept you not taking a big job because of me? It's not like we wouldn't see each other!" I screamed at him.

"We wouldn't see each other." The muscles in his forearm tensed, along with the rest of his body. He kept his eyes on the road. "It's a federal job with an undercover task force in Indiana."

My jaw dropped along with my heart. My brows rose. My mouth went dry. I felt like I had swallowed a spoonful of sand.

"Emma Lee." He threw the cruiser in park and turned toward me.

After I realized we were back at the funeral home, I jumped out.

"Emma!" he called after me.

I didn't turn around. I needed time to myself. I couldn't believe he was offered a big job and didn't tell me about it. By the conversation with his mom, I could tell he was still considering it.

"Emma Lee, let's talk about this!" he yelled louder.

I slammed the door of the funeral home. That was as far as I got. I pulled back the curtain on the window next to the door and watched Jack Henry. I couldn't believe he was contemplating whether or not to come in. I prayed he didn't. I had been humiliated enough tonight. Not only had I made a fool out of myself with the dog, I'd had no idea Jack Henry had been offered a big undercover job. My ego was bruised, and I needed time to think about how I was going to do the right thing. Let him go.

The idea of it brought tears to my eyes. Most teenage girls had posters of hot Hollywood celebrities on their walls. Not me. Every year I was in high school, I saved my allowance and bought two yearbooks. I used one to cut out all the photos of Jack Henry and plaster them on my wall. I used the other for what few friends I had to sign, trying to fit in and not be the "creepy funeral-home girl."

I wasn't one who needed to be made over, nor did I want him to beg me to talk to him. He knew me. He knew I needed time. Granted, I would be ready to talk to him tomorrow, but for tonight, I wanted to be alone.

"That boy loves you." Mamie Sue Preston stood behind me, looking over my shoulder.

In silence we watched the cruiser headlights pull out of Eternal Slumber's driveway.

"Come on." I walked back to my efficiency.

It was time I took care of Mamie Sue. Jack Henry might have left for the night, but tomorrow he'd be all over me about my new Betweener client and what I knew.

It was funny how my relationship with Jack Henry had started when I'd gone to him about my first Betweener client. We were able to separate business from pleasure. I was sure tomorrow he would show up at my door in business mode.

I grabbed the Baggie with Mamie's teeth, along with the hearse keys. I had a date with a grave-stone.

My daddy always told me to keep an emergency kit in the back of the hearse. When he and Mom moved to Florida, he gave me the kit, since I was taking over his part of the job. Mom had had the cushy job like Charlotte Rae.

My kit included a flashlight, extra batteries, hammer, screwdriver, blanket, jumper cables, tire gauge, bottled water, and a bag of trail mix, which had to be outdated by now.

The tools might seem strange, but you never know when a casket decides not to work properly or there might be a screw loose that needs to be tightened. Sounds strange, but, like everything in life, shit happens.

The Sleepy Hollow cemetery was locked up at night. We didn't have a caretaker who lived on the grounds, so it would be easy to slip in even if I wasn't in a hearse. Thankfully I had a key to the gate for emergency purposes. I was one of three who had a key. The city, O'Dell Burns and me. At times it was good to be an undertaker, and now was one of them.

I got the gate open and pulled in. I got back out to lock the gate back up. I didn't want any unwanted visitors in there, nor did I want someone to see the gate was open and call the police.

The headstones lined both sides of the road. Several different roads forked off the main one, but I kept going straight because Mamie was in the old section of the cemetery.

She sat still in the passenger seat with her hands neatly folded in her lap.

"You know . . ." She looked out the window. Her voice was almost a whisper. ". . . I'm not sure why anyone would want to kill me. I never bothered a soul. I was a pillar of the community."

"I'm sorry. People do mean things for no reason." I still didn't have a clear picture of a motive unless it was money. "Why did you leave money to the church?"

"Why not?" she asked back.

"I have never seen them do anything to acknowledge it," I said.

"Maybe I didn't want it to be acknowledged. Maybe they don't know it was me." She said a lot without saying a lot.

"Anonymous?" I asked.

"You can say that." She pulled back her shoulders and straightened up a little when we got to her stone. "Like I told you earlier, it was mine to do with what I wanted."

It was refreshing to know Mamie donated a large sum of money to the church. Granny was wrong about Mamie Sue. But I wasn't about to tell Granny that.

I grabbed the Baggie with Mamie's teeth in it and my bag of tricks from the back of the hearse and walked over to her stone. She was propped back on top with her legs crossed, like she was when I first saw her.

"I do love this bell." She flicked it a few times with her finger.

The sun had set and dusk was upon us, making it difficult to see the small hole where the bell string disappeared. I took the flashlight out of the bag and shone it on the hole.

"You know." Mamie paused and hopped off the stone. She ran her palm over the top of her name. "It's strange seeing my grave."

"I'm sorry." I had a strange feeling I needed to tell her how sorry I was she was murdered and how no one ever deserved to be killed.

"Enough about that." She waved her bony hands in the air. "Get to my teeth."

"Gross." My nose curled when I took the teeth out of the bag. "Are you sure this is going to work?"

I didn't know what happened to the dead once I got them six feet under, and I didn't care. Evidently they took the items in their casket with them to the other side.

"Positive." She rubbed her hands together in anticipation. "Now, get them in that hole." She instructed me, pointing to the dime-sized hole.

"The hole is tiny." I manipulated the end of the teeth in the opening. The teeth were much larger than the hole. "Does this hole go all the way into your casket?"

Suddenly I felt like I should have done more research on this type of casket setup.

"The hole into the casket is bigger." She did a shimmy shake. "All sorts of bugs can get in there, but I didn't care as long as I had that bell."

She shooed me to continue to try to get the teeth in the hole. No matter how many times I jabbed, turned, and thought, the teeth weren't going to fit.

"Use your hammer to make the hole bigger and wiggle them in." Mamie swung her legs and tapped the kit with her cane.

The hammer wasn't going to work because I would tear up the stone, then I'd get in trouble for messing with a corpse, which was illegal. I could use the screwdriver.

I put the tip of the screwdriver on the edge of the marble hole and slowly chiseled the hole until it was big enough to get the tip of the teeth in it. I wiggled the teeth until they finally dropped entirely underground.

"We did it!" Excitement filled me, and I looked up at Mamie.

"We sure did." She smiled with the biggest and

brightest teeth I had ever seen on a ghost. "Aren't they gorgeous?" She moved her head side to side with her mouth wide open. "I paid good money for these babies."

"You look beautiful." I smiled.

"Oh, ah, oh, ah." She opened her mouth and closed it several times, letting out an ominous sound.

Her hands pulled and tugged on the skin on her neck as though she was stretching it, then she put her fingers on her cheeks and moved them around in a circular motion, as if she were exercising her face.

"It's a bitch getting old and getting saggy skin." She opened her mouth really wide and closed it a couple times. "I spent a lot of money on beauty products to keep this skin tight."

The moon decided to come out. It shone down like a spotlight. I walked over to Mamie and took a good look at her.

"You look great as a ghost." I noticed she had much tighter skin than most women her age.

"I could use my face cream." Her eyes slid to me.

"Forget it." I shook my head and gathered my kit. "I got your teeth in there, I'm not putting facial cream down there."

The entire way back to the funeral home, I

couldn't help but smile. The only thing I could see in the dark was Mamie Sue Preston's teeth from her smiling the entire way home.

My argument with Jack Henry played over in my head, making it hard for me to even think about going to sleep that night. Mamie Sue disappeared, and I could only imagine she was enjoying having her teeth back in her mouth. It was only ten o'clock. Instead of trying to force myself to go to sleep, I decided to write down the pieces of Mamie's life and how they fit together, in order to help me find her killer.

I wrote, "Mamie Sue Preston was the wealthiest woman in Sleepy Hollow. How did she get her money? She died a virgin. She had a maid, Dixie Dunn, who she left her estate to. Why would she leave her big house to her maid?"

"Dixie Dunn." I tapped the name with my pencil. "Dixie Dunn holds the answers."

It seemed Dixie Dunn had had the most to gain from Mamie Sue dying, so I stuck her on the top of my list.

I glanced at the clock. It wasn't good manners to make social calls at ten o'clock at night, but who said I had good manners?

The full moon hung high on my way back to Mamie's fancy neighborhood. I had never been to

Beulah's home, and the address on the Auxiliary invitation was not too far from Mamie's mansion.

Beulah Paige's house was dark. I didn't see her fancy red Cadillac in her driveway, though it was probably in her detached garage, which was a mini version of her house. Mini, meaning it was as big as Eternal Slumber.

The front porch light flipped on after I beat on the door for a few minutes.

"Who is here at this hour?" Beulah's voice asked but the face didn't match Beulah's. "Emma Lee, do you know what time it is?"

"What happened to your face?" My eyes squinted. Maybe it was the lighting making her face so white. "Did you lose your tan?"

Beulah Paige was the Queen of Fake. Fake smile, fake niceness, fake eyelashes, and fake tan.

"What do you want?" she asked. *Want* came out as "wunt" with her disgusted tone of voice.

She shifted. Her black silk robe with the leopard fur around the edges hiked up on her full hips, lifting it above her ankles. In true Beulah fashion, she had on low-heeled slippers with a leopard puff on the top.

"I want to know what is on your face," I said.

She was scary-looking. The heavy white cream she was wearing looked like the same stuff

Granny made Momma smear on my nose when we went to the swimming pool when I was a kid. Up against Beulah's red hair, it made her look like a clown. I didn't like clowns.

"It's my night cream to keep the wrinkles at bay." She huffed and held the door tight against her body. "Go home. I need my beauty sleep. I will see you here tomorrow night. Not that I'm looking forward to it."

She went to shut the door. I put my hand on it to stop it.

"I wanted to ask you a couple of questions about Dixie." I put my toe on the bottom of the door so she couldn't slam it in my face.

"What on earth do you want to know at ten o'clock at night?" she asked.

"Who did she work for before?" I asked.

"I don't know or care." She blinked her black lashes. They were so long that she blinked cream right on them. "Good night."

She tried to shut the door, and we played the tango game, where I stopped her.

"Is she a business, or does she just work for herself?" I asked.

Beulah let out a big sigh. "Emma Lee, I'm tired. Don't mistake my accent for ignorance. Why are you here?"

"Charlotte Rae is on my ass about getting a person who can clean, and when I met Dixie at Junior's funeral, I thought she might have some friends or work for some company I can call." This lying stuff was getting easier and easier.

"I pay her under the table. The only thing I know is she shows up at seven in the morning and leaves around seven at night." Her foot slid out from underneath her robe. Gently she tapped it on the tile floor. "I guess I could find out, because your sister is definitely in need of an attitude adjustment."

"What?" I asked, wondering what had crawled up Beulah's butt.

"I gave her an invitation to the Auxiliary, and she snubbed me." Beulah drew in a breath. "The nerve thinking she is better than *me*."

She rolled her eyes and drew her hands to her chest at the same time.

"Oh." I smirked. "She does have an air about her. But, I wanted to know if I could get Dixie's contact information, since Charlotte's on me?"

"Hold on." She shut the door.

I heard the tapping of her shoes on the tile floor. Charlotte Rae had failed to mention the invitation. And it sort of made me mad. They were going to extend her an invitation and not me?

I pulled out of my thoughts when the door clicked open.

"You know." There was a puzzled look in her eyes. "I don't even have a number for her."

"How did you hire her?" I asked.

"There was this girl who came to the door telling me about her." Beulah bit her bottom lip, her brows crossed, as though she was thinking.

"A girl?" I asked. "What did the girl say?"

"She wanted to know if I had a cleaning lady, because she knew someone who cleaned the big house a few doors down." She leaned her body on her arm, holding on to the doorknob.

"A few doors down?" I knew she was talking about Mamie's, but Mamie had been dead for a while. Where had Dixie worked between Mamie and Beulah? *That* was the time frame I needed.

"People around here are always changing up their cleaning crew." She shrugged. "She offered me a deal. The next day Dixie showed up."

"Where was the girl?" I asked.

"I have no idea. I haven't seen her since." She rubbed her temples with her fingertips. "I need to go to bed. You are giving me a headache."

"Before I go"—I didn't budge—"are you sure Dixie isn't with a cleaning service?"

"I told you already. As long as she does a good

job, and judging by how fast everyone gobbled up the chess pie at Junior's repast, I'm thinking she's doing a fine job. I don't ask questions. You can ask her for some referrals tomorrow when you come back for the meeting, but you ain't taking her from me," she warned and waved her fingers in the air before she shut the door.

Seeing Beulah gave me more questions than answers. Now I wanted to know exactly who the first girl was who came to Beulah's door. She had to be part of Dusting Dixies.

Where had Dixie been for the past few years between Mamie and Beulah? Who did Mamie hang around with when she was alive? Who were her friends? According to her, no one, but everyone has to have at least one friend. What did Pastor Brown do with the million dollars?

Maybe the answers to some of the questions were the missing pieces I needed to figure out who'd had motive to kill Mamie. How did she die?

One thing I did know, I was going to be sitting in the front pew of Sleepy Hollow Baptist Church come sunrise.

Chapter 14

I think hell has just frozen over." Beulah Paige Bellefry hugged her Bible close to her chest when I passed her and the other Auxiliary women standing on the front steps of Sleepy Hollow Baptist Church.

"Amen," I cheered and stopped on their step. "Is this the greeting committee? Or is this a come to Jesus meeting?"

"That is not funny, Emma Lee. I don't have time to listen to your cockamamie bull malarkey today. I have a headache." Beulah Paige brushed her fancy gloved hands down her cream suit. She had a hot pink blouse underneath for a pop of color. "We are in the house of the Lord."

"Actually, we are outside." I stared at her eyes.

There wasn't one wrinkle. That heavy moisturizer must be working, and there was no way I was going to tell her she looked good.

Granny nudged me. She gave me the stink-eye.

"What?" I shrugged and used my fingers to help fluff up her matted-down hair. "God doesn't have a sense of humor? You really need to carry a comb if you insist on using a tight helmet." I referred to the aviator leather helmet she tugged over her head instead of a hard helmet.

Granny's lips pinched together. She hugged her pocketbook a little tighter to her body.

Mable Claire, Hettie Bell and Cheryl Lynne Doyle laughed.

Ahem, Beulah cleared her throat. We all stepped aside to make way for all the other churchgoers who were walking into the sanctuary.

"Say," I leaned my head and glanced over at the side entrance of the church. "Isn't that your maid?"

"I'll be," Beulah sucked in a breath and smiled. "I invited her, and I'm glad she decided to come."

We all went inside. I made sure I got a bulletin and walked down the main aisle to the front. The pews on both sides were full from the front to the back. It was like social time. Everyone with a happy face, greeting everyone.

There were a lot of people I didn't know and a lot of people I did. The stares from people I didn't know didn't bother me. The stares from people I did know bothered me.

"Deep in the valley the stone rolled away!" a voice sang out. It was familiar.

I looked but didn't see who was singing when service hadn't even started.

Granny grabbed my elbow and nodded her head to the front. Doc Clyde and Ina Claire were sitting in the front pew. I would get a good view right up Pastor Brown's nostrils.

"The stone rolled away!" The singing voice was closer. "Rolled away!"

The expressions on Doc Clyde's and Ina Claire's faces were indescribable. If I wasn't mistaken, I thought Ina Claire was looking up to the heavens to make sure a lightning bolt didn't come down and strike me dead when I sat down next to her.

"Amen," I leaned over to her and whispered.

She harrumphed and kept her eyes straight ahead.

"Deep in the valley the stone rolled away!" The voice was louder.

"Who is that singing off key?" I laughed.

"What?" Doc Clyde leaned around Granny and asked.

"That singing." I put my finger in my ear to block the noise.

"Yes." Doc Clyde slowly nodded his head. "The singing. Right, Zula Fae?"

Granny's entire body tensed. She cleared her throat and shimmied her butt into the pew, straightening her body.

"Rolled away!" the voice yelled.

I laughed. My eyes slid up to the altar. Mamie Lee stood in the choir line with her arms extended and head raised to high heaven, singing at the top of her lungs.

"Yes! Rolled away!" She dropped her head and skimmed the crowd.

"Sweet Jesus," I murmured when I realized the awful singing was coming right out of the mouth of Mamie Sue Preston and no one could hear her, leaving me looking crazy, yet again.

"Do you like the song?" Doc Clyde asked.

"What song?" I had to diffuse the crazy. "Are you okay, Doc? The service hasn't started yet."

"I told Eugene he needed to incorporate more music." Mamie watched as the choir filed in one by one with their purple robes on, leading into a song before Pastor Brown came out of the side door and took his seat on the altar.

Eugene? I looked at the bulletin and read "Pastor

Eugene Brown." Come to think of it, I had only known Pastor Brown as "Pastor Brown." I looked him over as he sat up there with his chin in the air. His blue eyes lit up as he preached the good word.

He did look like a Eugene.

Eugene glanced around the room. His eyes stopped when he got to me. He gave a hard squint as if he was making sure it was me. The crow's-feet deepened. They softened. Subtly his lips turned up to let me know of his approval.

Don't get used to it, Eugene, I thought and smiled back. He gave me the nod, *the Baptist nod.* The man had some secrets in there. I could probably sneak out all the gold in Fort Knox quicker than get those deep secrets out of Pastor Brown.

God forgive me, but I didn't listen to a word Pastor Eugene Brown preached on. I was too busy asking God to give me the answers to where the one million dollars was, because the financial report on the back of the church bulletin said the church brought in six hundred dollars last week and four hundred and fifty the week before that, which didn't come near to adding up to a million dollars.

One Sunday service wasn't going to get me the answers I needed.

I shifted in the hard pew, making a mental note on how he could spend a little of the million on pew cushions.

Pastor Brown asked everyone to bow their heads for the last prayer. I glanced over at Granny. Her eyes were shut as tight as bark on a tree, her hands folded in her lap. Her Bible was open to the day's scripture reading.

Sticking out of her Bible was a picture. I pulled it out gently so as not to disturb her prayer time. Her hand flew up and smacked the back of my hand. I still got the picture though.

"I'll be," Mamie Sue Preston said out loud. "I had forgotten all about that."

The picture was of two young women and a young man. They each had on pearls, long dark dresses, and the fanciest high-heeled shoes I'd ever seen. The young man was dapper in his black suit and fancy two-toned shoes. The picture was black and white, but the wealth of the three was apparent.

They were hugging on each other, standing on the steps of none other than the Sleepy Hollow Baptist Church.

Granny winked one eye open. She pointed to the girl on the far left and mouthed, "That was me at your age."

"And that was me." Mamie's finger came over my shoulder and tapped the other girl. "But that old bat ain't going to tell you that."

Granny and Mamie had been friends, and neither of them wanted to admit it.

I furrowed my brows and pointed to the other girl.

Granny shrugged and mouthed, "I can't remember." Her brow twitched. It was a sure sign she was lying to me.

"You are such an old goat. Can't remember my ass," Mamie belted over Pastor Brown's amen.

I snorted trying not to laugh. Granny dug her fingernails into my leg, only making me yelp. Pastor Brown looked at me.

"Don't forget about the spaghetti dinner on Wednesday night and keeping the good Lord's house in your giving today when you leave." He pointed to the back of the church. "A few of the deacons are back there with the collection plates."

The organist flung her fingers on the keys and belted out a Hallelujah before the congregation got up to leave.

"Who is that?" I pointed to the man.

"Honey," Granny smiled, "that is Pastor Brown when he was your age too."

"Emma Lee," someone said, touching my shoulder.

I turned around to find Pastor Brown staring at me.

"It was so good to see you this morning." He smiled. The eyes of the young man in the photo were the exact same eyes as Pastor's. "I'm sure it not only warmed Zula Fae's and God's hearts, but it made their week."

"Thank you," I said and noticed the line of people who were waiting to talk to him.

"I hope you come back." He patted me on the back.

"Pastor," Mable Claire interrupted. "I'm not going to be able to count the money tomorrow. I've got to be somewhere, and I just can't be in two places at once."

I watched her scurry off.

"What kind of money counting?" I asked.

"Mable Claire volunteers every week to count the collection plate. She also takes the money to the bank for me. She does a fine job," he boasted about her ability.

"I could do it one time." One time was all I needed to get some of the answers I was seeking. "I mean, I do the funeral home's money, and I don't mind offering my services."

"I'm thrilled to see you take an active role in the church." Pastor Brown rocked back and forth on his heels. "Can you be here in the morning?"

"Bright and early," I said.

That was settled. Everyone seemed happy. Everyone but Granny.

"What was that about?" she asked me in the parking lot of the church. She snapped the helmet off the handlebars of her scooter and rolled it down over her head.

"What?" I asked.

"You know what." Her words were sharp and held some anger in them. She snugged the aviator goggles over her eyes, magnifying them ten times their normal size.

"You've been trying to get me to go to church since I was legal enough to make my own decision not to," I said as I steadied the moped for her as she swung a leg over it.

She scooted her butt up to the top of the seat.

"You are up to something, Emma Lee Raines." She turned the key. "And I'm gonna find out." She twisted the throttle and whizzed off toward the Inn.

Chapter 15

Fluggie Callahan had done a big write-up in the paper about the revival of the softball league, and everyone was excited.

When I pulled into the gravel lot of Softball Junction I knew John Howard's idea was a hit. Who knew so many people had time on their hands, especially on a Sunday afternoon?

"Like the shirts, Emma Lee?" John Howard asked.

A lanky, blond-haired young man with dopey gray eyes and a wisp of a goatee stood next to him with a Grave Digger shirt on.

"I do." I nodded, putting my hand over my eyes to shield the sun. "Grave Diggers," I said in my best spooky voice. "Nice name."

"Thanks." John Howard's dingy hand smacked the boy next to him. "This here is Arley Burgin. He is my buddy who works for Hardgrove Funeral Homes."

Homes as in many.

"You know 'em?" Arley asked.

"Yes," I said without a hint of sarcasm, which surprised even myself.

Gina Marie Hardgrove. Saying her name put a bad taste in my mouth. My mind traveled back to mortuary school. I spent many wasted hours in Descriptive Pathology class gawking at the baseball-sized diamond on her hand—I blamed my C-minus on that ring. Needless to say, Charlotte Rae and I didn't have it easy, like Gina Marie. Everyone in the state knew the Hardgrove Funeral Homes. They started out in a neighboring town but quickly expanded throughout Kentucky. They weren't only a funeral home, they were also a reception center.

In one room, you could have a viewing of a dead client, and in another room they were celebrating the arrival of an impending birth. They ushered in births and sent out the dead. It was the darndest thing I had ever heard of. People loved it. Even brides started to rent out the reception hall. Talk about freaky.

"She's my boss," Arley said in a deep Southern accent, bordering the line of hillbilly.

"Boss?" That grabbed my attention real fast. I cocked my head to the side so I could hear Arley really well.

"Yeah, old man Hardgrove retired about six months ago, leaving Gina Marie, Ms. Hardgrove, in charge." He scratched his goatee. "Her brothers didn't like it too much."

"Really?" I asked.

Now *that* was some Southern fried gossip I could chew on. Charlotte Rae would find it very interesting, since those boys had spent a lot of time trying to get her to go out with them when we were younger.

My parents and Granny used to take us to conventions. Of course like anything else, the funeral world was just as small as Sleepy Hollow. We saw the same families, same kids and heard all the shared stories time after time.

The Hardgroves always fancied themselves rich. The boys especially strutted around Charlotte Rae like horny roosters, since she was the prettier, more endowed of the two of us. Granny scooted those boys off a dozen times at those conventions as they sniffed around Charlotte. I was sure one of them was eventually going to piss on her to mark his territory.

Granny always reminded me and Charlotte Rae to never forget our raisin'. Which meant never forget where you came from and it should keep you humble. I never forgot. Hell, who knew what happened to Charlotte Rae.

"Why yes, ma'am, she sure is." He took his Grave Digger hat off and rubbed his tangled, shoulder-length hair. "Them boys sure are mad. Mad as a wet cat. Mad." He shook his head and walked off with John Howard to the field.

I *bet* those Hardgrove boys were mad. They promised Charlotte Rae the world, saying they were going to be known as the Funeral Kings one day and would put her up in a mighty big house with all the finest things.

I recalled Charlotte Rae liking Gina Marie's big diamond too, and she did mention she could have one if she wanted to marry a Hardgrove.

Yeah, right.

Not with the bit of news I just got. I couldn't wait to tell Charlotte Rae about Gina Marie dethroning the Hardgrove kings.

"Hello, Emma Lee." Fluggie Callahan stood next to the fence with her camera at the ready, taking pictures of all the men in their uniforms. "Grave Diggers? Couldn't they come up with a better name?"

"I guess not." I looked out onto the field at my sponsored team.

My heart fell into my feet when I saw Jack Henry Ross out there in his tight white baseball pants and lime-green Grave Digger shirt. On the back they had ETERNAL SLUMBER printed on them.

His muscles contracted with every throw. Every time he caught the softball, it made a smack in his glove. I was thrown back into high-school mode all over again. Then I used to watch him from the sidelines and picture me running up to him at home plate after he made a home run. Today I felt the same.

I had no idea where we stood after last night's dinner with his parents that never ended up happening. And the fact I had found out he had been offered a job out of state and never once told me. Plus I knew he was considering taking it.

"Emma!" Jack Henry called out, waving his glove in the air, bringing me out of my memories. "Hi!"

His smile was boyishly affectionate. I waved and smiled back. I wanted him to have a good game. His attitude told me he still wanted to talk about what had happened. Today I was ready to conquer that beast.

Plus I was sure he wanted to question me about

Mamie Sue. If I could prove she was murdered and had enough supporting evidence, he'd be willing to exhume her body by going through the proper channels, Burns being one of them. But I had to give him reasonable cause.

Unfortunately, I didn't have the answers to his questions.

The umpires yelled for the game to get going. Grave Diggers ran into their dugout before they ran back out, taking the field first. We were up against Holy Bats from the Sleepy Hollow Baptist Church. Pastor Brown was up first.

"Hey, batter, batter, batter!" Grave Diggers screamed. They had their cleated feet propped up on the edge of the dugout, and their fingers grasped the chain fence. "Swing!" they yelled as soon as Vernon Baxter pitched the ball straight for home plate.

Pastor Brown made contact with the ball, sending it straight out to right field.

"Catch it, Jack Henry!" I screamed and jumped up and down in the stands.

Jack Henry caught it and the crowd went crazy. My heart swelled with pride.

"Everyone is having such a great time." Hettie Bell climbed to the top of the stands and sat down next to me.

She looked cute in her cutoff jeans, tank top and sandals. Her bob was pulled back on the sides with clips.

Each hand held a large Styrofoam cup.

"It's fun." I pointed to one of the church deacons, who was up to bat next.

"I got you a Diet Coke." She handed me the cup. "I figured it's your form of relaxation over yoga."

"Thanks, girl." I took it and sucked down a big gulp just as O'Dell Burns hit a bunt.

Vernon Baxter ran up between home plate and the pitcher's mound to grab the ball. He threw it to John Howard Lloyd, who was at first.

In the flash of an eye, I saw the base move to the right. I blinked my eyes. The base moved a little more to the right.

The deacon and John Howard danced around each other to see who could get to the base first.

If I didn't know better, I would have thought it was Mamie Sue's ghost playing a joke, but it wasn't. She was sitting next to me laughing so hard, I thought she was going to fall off the top bleacher.

"Emma!" someone screamed from the field. My eyes slid over to where it was coming from.

"Oh shit," I said.

Junior Mullins kicked the first base bag one more time before the deacon and John Howard fell on top of each other. Junior grinned ear to ear, smoke coming out the top of his head.

"That's what you get for setting my toupee on fire!" Junior waved his fist in the air at John Howard.

"Are you okay? Are they okay?" Hettie Bell didn't know whether to laugh like the crowd was doing or cry. She put her hand over her mouth. "Did the base move?"

"I don't think so." I took another swig of Diet Coke to help ease the pain of seeing Junior.

Seeing Junior meant one thing.

"Oh yes it did." Mamie smacked her hands together. "I swear. Junior Mullins was always playing tricks. He is so funny."

Ahem, I cleared my throat to keep back the tears. I wanted to run away. This job as a Betweener was getting harder and harder to deal with. They made me feel crazy.

"How do you do, Emma Lee?" Junior waved his hands from right field, where Jack Henry was staring at me. He looked like a smokestack standing out there.

By the look in Jack Henry's eyes, I could tell he knew it wasn't just by coincidence John Howard and O'Dell had collided. The umpires called the deacon out and the game continued.

Slowly, I shook my head to let both Jack Henry and Junior know I acknowledged them. Needless to say, Junior ruined what little joy there was with Grave Diggers winning their season opener.

"We have to talk." Jack Henry ran off the field and grabbed me by the arm before I could get the hearse door unlocked. "And not just about us, though it's the important one I'd like to discuss first."

"I agree, we do need to talk. But right here isn't the place." I wanted to get over to the post office to stake out the P.O. boxes.

Sleepy Hollow's post office didn't hold normal hours for P.O. box owners. They were only open from 3:00 to 5:00 p.m. on Sundays. It was pretty darn close to 3:00 p.m.

"Fine. I'll come over," Jack Henry said with a stern face.

"It's not a good time." I fidgeted with my keys.

"When then?" he asked. "Please don't say tomorrow. I didn't sleep all night. I couldn't call because of your phone and I came by this morning, but you weren't there."

"I went to church."

"You what?" He smirked, knowing I never went to church.

"Yep, me getting a little religion," I said. He

didn't seem amused. "Fine. I have a couple errands to run, and then I'm going to the Auxiliary meeting at seven. You can come over after that."

"And be prepared to talk about the first base thing," he warned before he bent down and gave me a sweet kiss on the cheek. "I love you, Emma Lee. And it felt good seeing you in the stands today."

He walked away without expecting me to say *I love you* back, even though I did. Unfortunately, I didn't want my heart to get any more broken when he told me he was going to be moving away from me. Far away.

"Jack Henry," Pastor Brown called as he ran after him. "I need to report something."

That got my attention. I meandered my way over to them, like my conversation with Jack Henry wasn't over.

"One of the collection plates is missing," he said.

"What do you mean?" Jack Henry asked.

"At the end of service we collect the offering. Then the deacons put all the money collected into one big collection plate. They lock it up. I count it and leave it for Mable Claire to count on Monday mornings before she takes it to the bank for a check and balance, keeping everyone accountable type of thing." He went on to say how the deacons had done their job. He'd gone in to count the money. He'd gone to the bathroom, and when he'd come back, the collection plate full of money had disappeared.

"Why don't you follow me down to the station and I'll get you to give a formal statement."

Pastor Brown agreed.

"Weird stuff is happening around Sleepy Hollow," Jack Henry said to me after Pastor Brown walked off to his car. "You and your little friends don't know anything about it, do you?"

"No." My brows wrinkled with contemplation. "No. What else is happening?"

"Artie has been coming into his store in the mornings and finding someone has been combining the fruits and vegetables. His surveillance isn't showing anything. Sanford Brumfield's goats are getting out again, and he even has surveillance. Nothing." He sighed. "I guess I'm going to have to get more patrols out."

I glanced over at the hearse. Mamie and Junior, his head still smoking, were standing there looking back at me. I wasn't so sure those two were quite so innocent.

"See you tonight." I reached for Jack Henry's hands and squeezed them before I darted back to the car.

"Spill it," I told them when I had safely pulled

away from any traffic that might see me talking to myself. "Why are you here, Junior?"

"It's as simple as this." Junior rested his elbows on the long front seat of the hearse, his body leaned up from the back. "Someone in that home of the near dead killed me. I told my family not to stick me in there, because once you go in, with your faculties or not, you don't leave. 'Home of the near dead' is what I call it. So you better saddle up with Jack Henry and get to making babies so they can take care of you when you are older, not stick you in some home. Or die alone, like Mamie Sue here."

Mamie nodded in agreement.

"Someone killed you too?" I groaned.

This was becoming a habit. The last Betweener clients were a pair. Died different times like these two, but still the same murderer. I wondered if Junior and Mamie had had the same killer. If so, what did they have in common besides the fact that both of them had been older?

"Yep."

"Do you know who did it?"

"Now, if I knew who killed me, I'd be over at their house scaring the shit out of them. I've already torn up Artie's Meat and Deli because he was always a jerk when I went in there." Junior was a feisty one. He was so thin, his eyes were buggy. He pointed to his head. "I outta spook John Howard again for setting me on fire."

"Is that thing going to smoke all the time?" I waved my hand in the air to clear the smell of burning fake hair.

"Hell, I don't know." He leaned back and looked out the window.

"You need to leave Artie's alone," I warned him.

"Y'all be nice! Ya hear!" Mamie chirped in. "Emma Lee, don't you go and work on his murder before you work on mine because you don't like the smell of burning hair. I was here first," Mamie protested.

"Now listen here." Junior scooted back toward the front. "I'm ready to go to the other side, now get me there."

"Shut up!" I screamed as the two bantered back and forth. "I'm going to try to figure out who killed Mamie first, because she was first. Junior"—I looked in my rearview mirror at the displeasure on his face—"you are going to have to take a number."

I glanced around to look at him. I felt like I was going to throw up when I saw a shadow of another ghost next to him.

Chapter 16

The P.O. box stakeout ended up being a bust. No one showed up to check his or her P.O. box. I didn't know whom I was expecting—Dixie Dunn or Emmitt Moss. The shadow I had seen in the back of the hearse must've been Junior's, because it wasn't there when I pulled into the post office.

I took the time to ask some questions.

"Mamie, do you know anyone who knew Junior?" I asked. "Or any reason someone would want to kill him?"

"Not that I know of," she said.

"Not that you know of." I pondered her answer and then asked Junior the same thing.

"No. I lived in the home of the near dead. Not some fancy rich person's palace." His brows furrowed, his arms crossed. He looked out the window. "And I was pretty popular too." He huffed.

"I'm trying to figure out if you had the same killer or if there are two different killers out there." I tried to recall any of the murder plots I had caught on *CSI* or even old Sherlock Holmes novels I had read.

"What is the last thing you remember?" I turned to Mamie.

"The last thing I remember was getting ready for bed. I had been gone all day at a charity event. I walked into my bathroom, washed my face, brushed my teeth and went back into my bedroom to put my nightclothes on." She had a distant look on her face. "I was really tired. Just really tired. I lay down on the bed without changing, and next thing I know, I was stuck between worlds." She smiled. "Then you came along."

"Did you eat at the charity?"

"Just the standard fare. Relish tray, fruit, and things like that. I did have a cocktail . . ." Her eyes narrowed, "Or two."

There wasn't anything out of the ordinary.

"Did everyone else eat the same things?"

She nodded.

"What about Dixie Dunn? Did she go with

you?" I knew it was a loaded question, so I anxiously awaited her answer.

Dixie was the only person who had access to all of Mamie's things, both while she was living and now, in the afterlife.

"Dixie Dunn is the kindest woman in the world." She shook her crooked finger at me. "If you think she tried to kill me, you get that out of your head, because she took care of me. Good care of me!"

Mamie Sue disappeared.

"Someone got mad," Junior said.

"If you and Mamie expect me to help you, I'm going to have to ask questions about important people you love and who were in your life," I warned him. "And for some reason, I can't put a finger on who would want to kill her. Even for her money. She seemed nice to everyone."

I kept the information about Dixie and Emmitt to myself. There was no need to tell a ghost when there was nothing he could do and he didn't know these people.

"Okay." I let out a heavy sigh, wishing I had my phone so I could take notes. "Tell me everything about your last living day."

"Well." He paused. "I got up. Got a shower. Got dressed."

"Big events." I wasn't going to waste my time on when he went to the bathroom.

"You said tell you everything," he said in a snide tone. "Fine. I went down to breakfast, which happened to be biscuits and homemade sausage gravy." He licked his lips. "I went back up to watch *Price Is Right.*"

I motioned him to go on.

"Fine, fine." He stopped. "I might've taken a little siesta or three before dinner. After dinner I got back up, put on my poker hat. It was the last thing I remember." He shrugged.

The day I'd gotten the call from the Happy Times Retirement Community about Junior's passing didn't strike me as odd, since I get a lot of business from nursing homes. Just like me, everyone thought he had died of natural causes, like most of the residents there. Jack Henry had come to take the report before I'd taken the body. Vernon Baxter had done the coroner's report, and he'd reported that Junior had died of natural causes, so there hadn't been an autopsy.

"Nothing out of the ordinary?" I asked.

"No, not a thing." He shook his head.

I put the hearse in gear when I realized it was after five and no one was coming to the post office.

I pondered Mamie and Junior's answers the entire way back to Eternal Slumber.

Jack Henry's cruiser was in front of the funeral home. He got out when I pulled in, and he followed me to the back of the lot where I had parked.

"I'm sorry." He took me into his arms as soon as I got out of the hearse. "I can't bear for you to be upset."

"I love you too, but I can't be the reason you don't live your dream," I whispered into his ear.

No wonder his mom didn't like me. She saw me as the one keeping him here in our small town, where there wasn't a whole lot of advancement in the police department. Jack Henry had already gotten the head job as sheriff, and there wasn't much more he could do.

"You are too talented to stay here." It was breaking my heart; I knew I had to do whatever I could to get him to take the job.

"I'm sorry you had to hear it from my mom." He pulled away and rolled his eyes. "Of all people."

"I think that was the hardest part," I admitted. "I guess I wish you had told me first. But I get it."

"I was going to tell you first, but she came to the office and saw the letter on my desk. And being nosy Jo Francis, she picked it up and read it. She insisted I take the job."

"Let's go in," I suggested. "We can talk while I get ready for the Auxiliary meeting."

We walked in, and before I could go all the way through the doorway, Jack Henry drew me close to him. He didn't need to tell me how he felt, he showed me.

Chapter 17

guess I can forgive you." I kissed his nose and jumped out of bed. "I've got to hurry up. I'm going to be late for my first meeting."

I was already ten minutes late, and the thought of how Beulah was going to react when I walked in made my stomach hurt. It would take me another ten minutes to get ready, and another ten minutes to drive there.

"Tell her I had to frisk you." His dimples deepened, and an evil grin crossed his lips.

"Jack Henry." I couldn't stop the smile. "You are a bad cop," I teased.

"Emma Lee, you will be the first person I tell when my decision is made about the job. In fact, before I make it, we will sit down and talk about the pros and cons." He propped himself up on the pillows in my bed. "Grab my jacket and look in the pocket. I've got you a gift."

"A gift?" I giggled. I loved getting gifts.

I grabbed his cop jacket and pulled out the packet in his pocket.

"I don't like not being able to get ahold of you," he said.

It was the latest and greatest smartphone. The one a small-town undertaker's salary wasn't able to afford.

"Oh, Jack Henry," I gasped. "This is way too much money for you to spend."

"Nah, the guy at the shop owed me a favor." He put his hand out. "Let me have it, and I'll turn it on so you can have it after you get ready."

"Thank you. I love it." I bent down and gave him a long, drawn-out kiss before handing the phone to him. "Now, what to wear."

I opened the door to my tiny closet and looked at the selection. The standard was going to have to work. A pair of black pants and a white button-down with some accessories. I didn't own pearls and diamonds like most of the women who were going to be there, so my large beaded multicol-ored necklace was going to have to do. It had just enough pop of color to make the outfit not look so funeral home-ish.

As I got ready, Jack Henry asked questions about Mamie.

"It's not just Mamie who is my new Betweener client." I didn't bother looking at him. I already knew the look I would get. "Junior Mullins is also here. Well, not here this minute. I have no idea where they go, but I do know Mamie gets mad at me when I ask her questions about her housekeeper, who happens to be the heir of her estate."

"Really?" Jack Henry sat up a little straighter.

"Yeah." I buttoned the shirt. "I found out Dixie Dunn had been her maid for years. Mamie left one million dollars to Sleepy Hollow Baptist Church and the rest in a trust for DD LLC, which belongs to Dixie Dunn."

"Does the lawyer in Lexington have anything to do with this?" He asked a question he already knew the answer to. I guess he just wanted to hear me confirm it.

"Yes. And I didn't tell him I was Bea Allen." I buttoned the sleeves before I walked over to my jewelry box and pulled out the necklace. "I told him I was with Burns to get any information on who would have paid Mamie's funeral bill."

"Did you go to the funeral home and take Bea Allen's pie?" he asked.

"No, but it was in Granny's garbage can. She said she didn't take it, and I do believe her." I pulled my brown hair over one shoulder and put the necklace around my neck before I headed over to the edge of the bed to let Jack Henry clip the clasp for me.

"Now the entire collection for Sleepy Hollow Baptist is missing." After he clasped my necklace, he pulled me to him, nibbling on the exposed skin on my neck. "You don't know anything about that?"

"Why on earth would I know anything?" I asked. "It's strange, because I was supposed to go and count the money tomorrow morning. I wonder if he still needs me, since it's all missing."

"It's like it vanished into thin air," Jack Henry said. "And what about the million dollars?"

"Strange. I asked Mamie about it because I haven't seen the church use any money that would amount to that." I took a swipe of mascara across my lashes and lip gloss on my lips. "She said people give money to churches all the time in their wills, which I know is true, but one million dollars?" I shrugged and made my way back over to give him a kiss good-bye. "Junior was murdered, and neither of them have a connection to each other."

"Hmm." Jack Henry's eyes lowered. "I wonder if some of the Happy Times workers knew something. It's always on the news how something fishy goes on in those places. I go by there every once in a while. Maybe I'll stop in."

"Yeah, I have plans to go check it out." I bit my lip.

"*I* will check it out. Not you. I guess I'm going to have to try to get him exhumed along with Mamie." His face hardened. "I hate doing that without some sort of concrete evidence."

"I'm trying." I knew he wasn't going to be happy with my amateur sleuthing techniques.

"I told you when you started this Betweener job to leave the cop stuff to me." He warned, "Don't you do any more. Emmitt Moss is already on to you, and so is Bea Allen. Thanks to my mom, Bea Allen isn't going to press charges against you, even though Mom said you were a little crazy."

"Great." I sucked in a deep breath and held my arms out. "Do I look like Auxiliary material?"

"Better." He smiled, then his face grew serious. "Please don't tell me you are doing this gossip group just to get information on Junior and Mamie or this Dixie Dunn character."

"Let's just say I want to pick Dixie Dunn's brain, since her new employer is Beulah Paige." I smirked and cocked a brow.

"Be careful. Whatever information you have, you bring to me and I'll look into it." He stared. "Got it?"

"Got it." I grabbed the new phone and headed out the door.

Chapter 18

I felt a lot better now that Jack Henry and I had made up. Granted, I didn't know where our relationship stood if he did take the job out of town, but he was here now, and that was good enough until something happened.

For now, I had to put my relationship issues on hold and sleuthing hat on to see what I could figure out about Dixie Dunn, on the down-low, of course.

The hearse looked out of place amongst the Volvos, Mercedes, and other luxury cars, but I didn't care. I pulled right up front in the center of the round driveway, smack dab in front of the steps. Business was business. Maybe I could get some pre-need arrangement applicants while

I was there, then maybe Charlotte Rae would change her mind about joining.

There was a fancy butler guy at the entrance with a tray of champagne flutes filled with the bubbly stuff.

"Ma'am?" He held the tray out at a good distance from his person, but not too far.

"Thank you." I carefully took a glass, fearing that if I took the wrong one, it would send the entire tray tumbling.

Evidently, he had done this a few times. The tray didn't even tilt.

"Right this way." Dixie Dunn appeared out of nowhere and gestured to follow her.

"Hi, Dixie." I looked around to see if anyone was nearby. There wasn't, so I took the opportunity to ask, "Do you remember me?"

"Yes, ma'am," she said in a whisper.

"I meant to get some information from you about hiring someone to clean the funeral home on a regular basis." Regular meaning once a month at the most. Other than that, Charlotte Rae would flip. "Are you available?"

"I'm full-time here, and sometimes I just stay overnight if I work late, but I can recommend someone." She eyed me. "I own a cleaning service and have several girls who work for me. I'll check

and get back with you. Tinsie"—Dixie grabbed
the arm of another girl with a Dusting Dixie
apron on—"Can you please get Miss . . ."

The girl looked at me. It was the same thin
young girl who answered the door at Mamie Sue's
private residence, only her unruly black hair was
slicked up into a tight bun, making her look like
a ballerina.

"Say," she snapped her fingers. "This is the girl
who came to the Preston house in a hearse."

I gulped down the big goose egg in my throat.

"I see." Dixie Dunn's eyes drew down me and
then back up. "Tinsie, can you please get her
number? I need one of the girls to go over to her
funeral home and get an estimate for our services."

"Dead people?" Tinsie's nose curled.

"Just get her number," Dixie ordered. She took
the tray of crackers and fancy cheese from Tinsie
and disappeared into a sea of bobbling heads of
gossipy women gathered in the all-season room
in the back of Beulah's house.

"Hold on." Tinsie held up a finger.

Only I didn't hold on. I waited until she went
into Beulah's kitchen and I darted up the steps. If
Dixie Dunn lived here at times, maybe she'd have
something in her room.

The largest room had to be Beulah's, and I

couldn't resist. The large mahogany posters on her bed—which was too high to just sit on—were as large around as the pillars on the front of her house. The covers were fluffy down, and it took every ounce of restraint in my body not to take a running dive into them.

This was the type of room I dreamed of. And the closet was just as large as the room. There was a fancy shoe rack in the middle with an electric spinner so Beulah didn't have to walk far or reach up to get the pair she wanted. Her clothes were arranged in color coordination. Attached to each outfit was a small velvet pouch with jewelry to go with it.

Damn, it must be nice to be rich. I walked out, through the room to the other side, and stepped through the other door.

"Oh my God." I walked into the room and sat my flute on the counter of the bathroom sink.

Beulah's bathroom had to be fancier than the Queen of England's. Her drapes were adorned with tassels and the shiniest silk. Since taking over the funeral home, I knew how much nice drapes cost, and these were not cheap.

The marble tub sat on gold clawed feet. One of those fancy rainfall heads dangled down from the ceiling, and every showerhead was angled to not leave one body part with a speck of dirt.

The marble counter was full of all sorts of beauty products. She had at least one hundred different bottles of perfume, ranging from Christian Dior to Chanel. The bottle stared at me, begging me to get a little squirt. Just a little tiny spray wouldn't hurt.

I admitted to perfume envy, since I was used to the death smell. And let's just say the death smell was real and was a far cry from Chanel. I couldn't help myself. I picked up the bottle and did a little dab behind my ears and on my wrists before returning it to its original spot.

"Oh," I picked up the moisturizer. She had at least ten bottles of the same one.

When I opened it, I noticed it had the same peach smell that had caught me off guard the night I had come by to see her . . . or rather, be nosy. It had to be the same stuff.

I stuck my finger in and rubbed a sample on the back of my hand. I lifted it to my nose and took a deep breath. The spot I rubbed it on looked moist and shiny.

"Is there something I can help you with?" Dixie Dunn stood behind me.

"I've got to poop." I held my hand to my stomach. "I didn't want to stink up the guest bathroom, and I knew Beulah wouldn't mind if I used her bathroom."

"Actually," Dixie Dunn plucked the moisturizer jar from me and put it back. "She does mind if you are anywhere in her home. She asked me to keep an eye on you, and I see she was right."

"I beg your pardon?" I pulled back like she had gotten it all wrong. Again, I didn't have a good poker face. "The nerve. After I pooped, I was washing my hands and saw all this moisturizer. I couldn't help but notice how good her skin looked at church this morning, and I wondered if this is what she's using."

"Yes. She loves this moisturizer. I actually make it from herbs and natural ingredients." Dixie's face lit up. Her eyes brightened. "It was my momma's secret cream."

"No! Don't be going around giving everyone your special cream!" Mamie Sue appeared and stuck her cane in Dixie's face.

"Tell me about it," I encouraged Dixie.

By the way Mamie Sue acted, maybe I was on to something.

"It's been in my family for years, like the chess pie I made the other day for Junior Mullins's repast." She opened a jar and took a swipe with her finger. She grabbed my arm and used both her hands to rub it in.

"That was my recipe," Mamie Sue muttered, and I realized it really wasn't.

"I've been making it on the side and selling it at different little boutiques in Lexington. It's a big seller." She stopped rubbing, keeping her hands on me. She looked me in the eyes. "Do you really see a difference in Beulah's appearance?"

"I do," I admitted. "How much does this cost?"

I was game for a jar. If it opened up a line of communication with Dixie.

"I'll give you a jar." She picked up one of Beulah's. "Take one of hers. She'll never know, and I'll just replace it. If you like it, tell all your friends, or even clients at the funeral home."

"My clients are dead," I reminded her. "But I can mention it to families."

"That would be wonderful. I'd love to grow the distribution and become larger than those fancy moisturizers, which are mostly water and not ingredients." She picked up another brand of moisturizer in a much fancier bottle than hers. "This stuff is crap." She put it back and rubbed her finger and thumb together. "Unfortunately, I need the cash to run with the big dogs."

"Really? How much?" I asked.

"A lot. More than a couple million to do it right. I guess I have to clean a lot more houses." She sighed. "We better get back before Beulah has my hide and yours."

Millions? I looked at the jar she'd given me. I had her motive for killing Mamie Sue. Now I needed the weapon. *You mean kill a lot more people?* I thought but kept my mouth shut.

Beulah had already scouted the house for us and found us coming down the large staircase.

"I told you she'd be all over this house." Hate dripped out of Beulah's mouth.

"No, ma'am, she has a bad case of the diarrhea." Dixie kept my lie. "And I told her she could use the upstairs guest bathroom."

I pinched my nose and fanned my other hand in front of my face.

"I wouldn't go up there if I were you." I doubled over like I was really sick.

"You need to leave if you are sick. I won't have the women get sick from your germs and blame my party for it." She stuck her arm out for me to go out the front door. "And why do you have a jar of my moisturizer in your hand?"

"Oh, it's not yours." Dixie Dunn came to my defense again. "I noticed she's got some premature wrinkles and told her about my cream. She bought a bottle."

"You are working for me right now. Not selling shit." Beulah's teeth gritted. "Get back to work. It was nice seeing you, Emma Lee."

She walked down the stairs and opened the front door. It was her polite way of throwing me out.

"There you are." Tinsie came into the room with a tray of small cocktail glasses filled with something really refreshing. She handed the tray to Beulah. "I need to get your number," she said to me.

"Are you kidding me?" Beulah's face contorted. It was apparent she was beneath holding a tray of food for her own party.

"I'm so sorry," Dixie profusely apologized for Tinsie's actions. "She's young and learning. It won't happen again."

Dixie took the tray from Beulah.

"You're damn right it won't. Send her home and don't let her step toe on my property again." Beulah took a quick turn and stormed out of the entryway.

"Get the number and go," Dixie instructed Tinsie.

I rattled off my number and Eternal Slumber's number before I left.

Chapter 19

It was a happy sight to see Jack Henry's cruiser still in the driveway of the funeral home when I got home.

I was hoping to get a little time with Mamie to ask her about Dixie Dunn's capital adventure in the beauty product department, but she didn't show herself, and neither did Junior. I wondered where they were and what they did when they weren't with me.

"You are home early." Jack Henry was laid out on the couch, remote in hand. He glanced at his watch. "I'm guessing it wasn't the beer-drinking kind of party, because you weren't gone long."

"No." I plopped down in the chair beside the couch. "But I did score some moisturizer."

"Moisturizer?" He shook his head.

"Yes. And I think I got my motive for Dixie Dunn to kill Mamie Sue Preston." I was pretty pleased with myself.

"There is no way on this earth Dixie killed me. No way." Mamie sat on the couch next to Jack Henry.

I glared at her. She was looking at him.

"What?" Jack Henry sat up. "Is one of them here?"

"Yes." I let out a heavy sigh. "Mamie, and she claims Dixie didn't kill her. But evidence is stacking up."

"Like what?" they both asked at the same time.

"Dixie Dunn was your maid and she needed the cash to make the beauty line; you left her the cash as the beneficiary of your estate." My brows lifted.

"She's been with me for years. I made her beneficiary a long time ago. She would've killed me then," Mamie said.

"Oh." I wasn't sure how to respond. She was right. What was Dixie's reason for waiting? "Maybe she waited until you were older and no one would suspect you got killed. Died of natural causes."

"Are you talking to her?" Jack Henry asked. "Because if you are, I'm going to finish watching the game." He used the remote to turn up the volume.

"Don't you care about this?" I asked him.

"Yes. I do. But she was buried with Burns. It's going to take an act of Congress to get Emmitt Moss to sign a release so I can get her body up and take a look at bones and dust." He shook his head.

"So you are just going to let my killer go unknown and leave me in the Between world?" Mamie cried out.

"No," I grumbled. "I'll find out who killed her."

"No, you won't." Jack Henry didn't bother looking at me. He kept his eyes on the TV. "It's not like there is some sort of serial killer out there."

"Are you sure?" I asked.

"Yeah. Are you sure, you little whippersnapper?" Mamie Sue wasn't happy with Jack Henry's performance as sheriff.

"Yes, Emma Lee. There are no serial killers in Sleepy Hollow," Jack Henry laughed.

Just then, a dispatch came across his police radio, which was attached to his uniform still balled up on my bedroom floor.

He rushed in the bedroom and came out fully dressed.

"Where are you going?" I asked. "I thought you were spending the night?"

"I'll be back." He kissed me on the forehead. "I'm heading over to Triple Thorn subdivision. It looks like Beulah Paige passed out during the Auxiliary meeting and is on life support."

My throat tightened. My chest hurt. Suddenly I became dizzy. I leaned up against the wall and only heard Jack Henry slam the door behind him.

I slid down the wall. My knees bent in the air, my hands flung out on either side, I couldn't move.

"Maybe now he will believe there is a serial killer around Sleepy Hollow." Mamie knelt down beside me. Her eyes were more hollow than I remembered them.

After I gathered my wits about me, I fixed myself a cup of coffee and waited for Jack Henry to come back. It seemed like forever, but in actuality it was only a couple of hours and rounding midnight before I heard his car pull up.

I greeted him at the door.

"I don't know what happened to her." He took his hat and rubbed his hand on the top of his head.

"Is she . . ." I hesitated to use the word *dead*.

"No, she's not dead." He paused. "Yet."

My stomach fell to my feet. "What happened?"

"After you left, I guess she was so worked up about you going into her room and taking a poop, she might've had a slight heart attack or something." He shrugged past me. "She complained of chest pains, a headache, and the next thing they knew. Wham!" He smacked his hands together. "She was on the ground."

"Oh my God." I took Jack Henry by the hand. "That is awful. I didn't do anything to put her one foot in the grave."

"When I took some statements, the maid— your killer . . ." He fumbled for her name, finally taking the notebook out of his pocket. He flipped it open and read, "Dunn, Dixie Dunn. According to Dixie, she was mad about you using the bathroom upstairs and how you were spreading your virus all over the place. Not to mention some face cream."

He put his hand on my head.

"I'm lovesick, nothing real sick. I told her that." I jerked my head away from his hand.

"So you were snooping around and she caught you." He had it all figured out. I nodded. "Then you started to mess around in her bathroom at all the pretties." I nodded, he continued. "Then you wanted to try the cream and did."

"Yes, but I didn't take any. I told you Dixie Dunn made the moisturizer and gave me a jar. She said she needed money to make a go of it. Millions."

Millions.

"Are you sure this Dixie Dunn gave you the cream, because I don't want Beulah Paige Bellefry coming back from this coma and accusing you of putting her there by stealing." He looked at me.

"Yes. Dixie Dunn gave me the jar." I pointed to the jar sitting on the table next to the couch. "There it is."

"But you did play pretty in her bathroom while pretending to be sick?" he asked.

"How do you figure all this stuff out?" I found it eerie.

"Because you smell delicious and I know that's not your original scent of Eau de Toilette of Death." He pulled me tight and gave me a big, long kiss to start off the rest of our night.

Chapter 20

I staggered out of bed to answer the phone Jack Henry had stuck on the dresser before he made his way to bed last night.

"Granny?" I answered frantically. My heartbeat rang out loud and clear in my ears. "What's wrong?"

Granny was an early riser, not an early caller.

"You have got to get over here right away," she cried out, a sudden fury in her voice. "Someone is trying to frame me."

"Frame you?" I eased back on the bed, trying to steady my pounding heart from her scaring me half to death.

Images of Beulah Paige danced in my head. Was someone figuring out I was snooping around and going after all my people? Not that Beulah

Paige was one of my closest friends, but we did run in the same Sleepy Hollow circle.

Jack Henry propped himself up on his elbows. Even his short, high-and-tight haircut was mussed up. He rubbed his eyes.

"Yes. Get over here." Granny hung up.

"I guess I need to run over to the Inn." I looked over at Jack Henry, who had fallen right back to sleep.

I didn't bother waking him up. If I needed him, I knew where to find him. I slipped on my Kentucky sweatshirt and khaki shorts before I darted out the door.

There wasn't time to drive over, so I hightailed it as fast as a jackrabbit across the square.

"Whoa! What's the hurry?" Junior Mullins glided along next to me, smoke trailing behind.

"I'm not sure. Something's wrong with Granny," I said, not caring a bit in the world who saw me talking to him.

"Like what?" he asked.

"She said someone's framing her." I jutted up the steps of the Inn, letting the screen door smack behind me.

"I didn't say murdering me or breaking in." Granny was in full regalia. Her hair was nicely styled, and she wore a pair of cropped jeans and a blue cardigan with a simple necklace that had a Z charm dangling from it.

She stood in the powder room off the hallway of the Inn, slathering white stuff all over her face.

"What is that?" I asked.

"New moisturizer from Beulah's maid." Granny must've thought the more the better. It was thick like plaster and if she smiled, her face might crack. "I guess you heard about Beulah. Damn shame I had to cook dinner last night for the Inn guests and not be there on time to see them cart off Beulah in the ambulance. But I did get there in time for the maid to sell everyone a jar of her fabulous cream."

I watched Granny rub the cement down her neck.

"I heard you put her into a frenzy when you had your bout of diarrhea." Granny's brows cocked. Too bad the paste didn't cover them. "Diarrhea? You were looking for something. I know you, Emma Lee."

"Granny, don't let your imagination run wild." I shook my head and stepped out of the door of the bathroom to make room for her. "What is this nonsense about being framed?"

I followed her into the kitchen. There was flour all over the floor, sugar spread all over the counter, and honey dripping down the lower cabinets.

"What happened?" I stayed at the door and looked in.

"That is what happened." Granny pointed to an overturned round bronze plate on the kitchen floor.

I bent down to take a look.

"Is there some sort of animal under it, because this place is a mess." I started to flip it over.

"Don't touch it!" Granny stopped me. "We need fingerprints."

"Fingerprints?" I bent down a little more. There were some words stamped in gold on the bottom. "Sleepy Hollow Baptist Church?"

I glanced back at Granny. Her eyes held a fear in them.

"Now." She took a gulp. "I've done a lot of underhanded, sneaky things in my life. But being a thief and stealing from God has never crossed my mind."

"The money?" I gasped. "Is that the collection from yesterday's service that went missing?"

"I swear, Emma Lee." Granny walked over and showed me what she had done. "I was happily making my biscuits and sausage gravy." Her brows lifted, cracking the plaster on her forehead. "My secret ingredient is honey. So I went to the cabinet and opened it to grab the honey."

She went through the motions. I eyed her Bible

sitting on the kitchen table. The more she talked, the more I wanted to get my hands on the picture of her, Mamie Sue and Pastor Brown.

"When I opened the cabinet, the honey was open and sitting in *that* plate." She jabbed her finger down toward the collection plate. "I just couldn't believe my eyes. I took the plate down, and when I looked down into it and saw all the money, I dropped it and called you."

"You didn't seem too upset when I came in with you spackling the white stuff all over your face," I said, trying to contemplate what I should do.

Call Jack Henry and tell him Granny had the money? Call Pastor Brown and explain we found it in the cabinet?

"I knew you were on your way and I couldn't dare stay in here with the money someone planted on me. Just like the pie." Her eyes narrowed, her lips thinned. "I bet Bea Allen is trying to get rid of me."

"No," I shook my head, "she's trying to get rid of me."

"What?" Granny's head almost twisted off her neck.

"Nothing." I didn't have the time or energy to go into detail about my disastrous date with Jack Henry at his family's home and Bea Allen flapping her lips about me impersonating her. "Let's just go over this one more time."

Granny did her entire routine, and nothing changed. When she made the motions of opening the cabinet and all the stuff falling to the ground, I pulled the picture out of Granny's Bible and stuck it in my pocket.

"When was the last time you opened the cabinet before this morning?" I asked.

There had to be some sort of reasonable explanation for Sleepy Hollow Baptist Church's entire collection being in Granny's cabinet with her honey sitting on top.

Okay . . . maybe not reasonable, but some sort of answer.

"Did you tell anyone about your secret ingredient of honey when making your biscuits?" I asked, trying to narrow down someone, anyone.

"No." She ran over to the ball of yeast she had covered over. She cried out, "Now these aren't going to be any good because I've waited too long to put honey on them."

"Granny," I said. "Focus."

"Focus? Are you kidding me?" Granny tossed the rising dough ball into the trashcan. "I have Inn guests who will be up in less than thirty minutes. I have all of Sleepy Hollow's residents' ten percent tithe drenched in honey on my floor. And someone placed Bea Allen's pie in my cabinet a couple days ago. Twice!" She held up two boney fingers. "Now this!"

"I have an idea." I picked up the plate, to Granny's displeasure.

There was a lot of money. Most of it was dripping in honey. I put the money in the sink and turned the faucet on.

"We are going to launder the money, literally?" Granny asked.

"No." I did my best cleaning off the honey. "You are going to take a chisel hammer to get that crap off your face. I'm going to sneak the money back into the church."

"How are you going to do that?" She put a hand on her hip.

"You are going to get rid of the plate, and I'm going to hide the money under my sweatshirt. Remember," I smiled, "I told Pastor Brown I would fill in for Mable Claire."

Mable Claire. Exactly why couldn't she volunteer today? I tucked the little question in the back of my mind with the rest of them.

Granny and I hatched our plan. She was going to put her finest Southern pearls on and do the best she could with the biscuits she was working on. I was going to grab a cup of coffee at Higher Grounds Café on my way to Sleepy Hollow Baptist Church to put the money back and do my volunteer duties.

I probably should've gotten a shower and brushed my teeth first, but the way I saw, God didn't care what I looked like as long as I returned the tithe. And maybe did a little snooping around for Mamie's million dollars.

"Good morning," I said to Mable Claire, who was sitting in her regular table at Higher Grounds, minus Beulah Paige. I stopped to give my condolences. "I'm so saddened to hear about Beulah. Is she going to be all right?"

"I don't think we should talk about it, since you were the one who put her there." Mable Claire's bottom lip jutted out.

"Mable Claire, I did no such thing," I protested, being careful not to move around too much with the wad of cash stuck down my waistband. "When I left there, she was healthy as a hog. Regardless, I wish no ill will on anyone."

"Thankfully she switched her funeral arrangements to Burns, and I'm going right over to do the same thing." Mable Claire stood up and jingled her way to the door.

"Good!" I yelled at her back. "We don't want

you anyway," I muttered, thinking about the hissy fit Charlotte Rae was going to have when she found out.

"Let's hope she doesn't kick the bucket." Cheryl Lynne poured a to-go cup of coffee for me. "It seems like you are batting a thousand with the Auxiliary women."

"Yeah," I grumbled and ran my hand through my hair, which was becoming increasingly greasy as the morning minutes flew by.

"I was there last night," she said. "I'm not sure you want some coffee with your bowel issues." She handed the cup over the glass-top counter.

"I don't have diarrhea." I knew what she was saying without having to say it. "I'm fine," I informed her.

"There seems to be a lot of strange things going on around here." Cheryl leaned against the glass counter, resting on her forearm. "The money from the church went missing. Beulah has some sort of heart attack. Strange."

"How did you know about the money from the church?" I asked. Jack Henry was pretty good at keeping police business on the down-low.

"Mable Claire told me." She pointed to Mable Claire, who was across the street on the sidewalk talking to Pastor Brown. Cheryl Lynne walked over to the cappuccino machine. She threw in all sorts of things to make the fancy drink. "I guess she should know. She comes in here every Monday morning before she goes to the church to count the money."

"She wasn't going today." I watched the interaction between Mable Claire and Pastor Brown.

"What did you say?" Cheryl Lynne asked over the cappuccino maker.

"Nothing." I waved and stood at the door of the café until Mable Claire and Pastor Brown turned enough so they wouldn't see me slip out and down the street to the church.

Haste makes waste, and I didn't wait. If fast walking was an Olympic sport, I knew I could win a gold. No one, not Pastor Brown, was going to beat me to the church. I would slip in through the side door, which was always open for anyone who felt the spirit and needed to pray, and put the money in a different collection plate.

All in Sleepy Hollow must have been good, because no one was in there to pray. I did stop at the altar and give a little healing thought to Beulah Paige. If she did have a heart attack because of me and my lies, that would be hard to live with. I really did want her to be okay, although maybe come back a little nicer.

"Boo!" Junior danced around, smoke signals floating up in the air. The signals turned into perfect smoke rings. "I've figured out how to create rings. If I move this way and that way . . ." He darted in a circular motion.

"Great." I walked up the altar steps and went over to the door Pastor Brown always comes out of during service, then I jiggled the handle.

To my surprise, it was open and exactly where I needed to be—the hallway, the guts of the church. On my way down the hall, I opened each door on the left and the right. I needed the office, and these were Sunday-school classrooms. Each had a table with chairs around them, Bibles on top, and a chalkboard with all sorts of Bible verses written on them. One of the rooms had a Baggie full of frosted animal crackers.

I couldn't resist. I took the bag.

"Mm . . ." I chewed on an animal cracker and sipped my coffee. It was so good.

The office was at the end of another hall. The door was open, so I was happy I wouldn't have been accused of breaking and entering. The empty collection plates were stacked on a large credenza.

The sound of footsteps caught my ear. I jumped in the rolling chair and took the money out of my waistband. I wheeled over to the credenza and stuck the wad of cash in the top collection plate. With the plate in my hand on my roll back to the desk, I grabbed a piece of paper off the copier and pencil off the desk.

"One hundred and twenty," I counted the money loud enough for the person coming closer to hear me. "Twenty-one, twenty-two." I wrote the number down. "Jesus loves me this I know," I sang and pretended to stack the money when I heard the footsteps stop at the door of the office.

"For the Bible tells me so." I sang loud and proud of the one and only song I remembered from Sunday school.

"Emma Lee?" Pastor Brown asked.

"Pastor." I smiled and held a stack of money in one hand. "I'm here to do my volunteer work."

"Where did you get the money?" he asked with a perplexed look on his face. He walked over. His mouth dropped when he saw the collection. "Where did it come from?"

"Um . . . in the plate right here." I tapped the stack with my pencil. "Is this not right?"

"You mean you came in here and the money was in the collection plate?" he asked with trepidation.

"Right there," I confirmed my big lie.

Please God, don't strike me dead right here in your house. I bit my lip and begged for forgiveness.

"Is everything all right?" I asked, as if I didn't know anything about the missing collection.

"Great!" He clasped his hands together. Joy spewed out of his mouth. "Better than great, Emma Lee!"

"Great." I shrugged and turned back around.

The sound of a cabinet opening caught my attention. Then Pastor Brown's footsteps.

"Here are the checks from the other collection." He handed me a stack of paper checks. "You will log the number on the check, who it's from, and the amount in this ledger."

I opened the notebook. Mable Claire's handwriting was clear and neat. After I counted the sticky money and put it in the zipper deposit bag, I worked on the checks. It was going to take me forever to do these. I worried about how much time I was going to have to snoop.

"Yes." I heard Pastor Brown talking to someone.

I bent back in the chair and looked through the open door he had disappeared through. He was sitting behind a desk, and the back of the chair was to the door. The phone cord left the receptionist-type phone and tugged around the chair.

"I came in and Emma Lee Raines was counting

the cash right here," he let the other person know. "Yes. Emma Lee. Mable Claire wasn't able to come today, so Emma had volunteered yesterday after church to come in and count it."

I smiled. I did kind of like him bragging on my volunteering until I figured out who it was he was talking to.

"Thanks, Jack Henry, for all your work. I must've not seen it in there. It's my fault." Pastor Brown said a few more words and hung up.

Great. Now Jack Henry was going to be on my ass about the money. He was way too smart to think Pastor Brown had misplaced the money and it had just shown up.

Quickly I got to the last check.

"Junior Mullins?" I asked and looked at the check. It was written when Junior was still living.

"Of course I pay my little tithe to the church." Junior appeared next to me, looking down at the check. "It might only be ten percent, but it's what the good book calls for."

"Excuse me?" Pastor Brown walked out of the office.

"This check is from Junior Mullins." I thought it was strange. "And for two thousand dollars?"

I gulped when I heard Junior say "ten percent." Wasn't ten percent a lot? Considering Junior had one of the cheapest funeral packages and lived in the old folks home, I figured he was on a fixed income.

"Two thousand dollars." Junior's face set. "Fine. I know it should've been three thousand, but I was afraid the home of the near dead was going to up my rent. Hell, I didn't know I was going to die."

"Emma Lee?" Pastor Brown's hand waved in front of me. "I hope you know people's tithe to the Lord is a private matter and this information doesn't leave the office." He took the check from my hand. "Mable Claire is very good at keeping every penny coming into the church discreet." He took the ledger and stack of money, along with the checks. "I hope I can count on you to do the same."

The image of them talking on the sidewalk this morning was stamped into my brain. Did Mable Claire know everything about the money coming in and out of this place? Just how much did Sleepy Hollow Baptist Church have?

One million dollars for sure. Where was it?

"Of course I won't say a word." I made the sign of the cross like Granny always did.

"Dear, we aren't Catholic. Your discretion is appreciated."

"Yes. Yes." I nodded. "But do the deceased members ever leave the church money in their wills?"

It seemed like a good question to start with.

"It's not unusual for them to leave the church a little something." He smiled. "After all, it all belongs to God. Have you ever seen a U-Haul behind a hearse?"

"No sir," I laughed. My first Betweener client, Ruthie Sue Payne, used to say that. "But what do you do with the money?"

"Pay bills, pay salaries. It's not cheap to run a church," he said.

"Salaries?" I guess I had always thought everyone did volunteer work.

"Sure. Mine." He pointed to himself. "The accountant. The lawyer. The secretary. Handymen. A bunch of people are on salary at the church, but no one in the community realizes that when they have a hard time paying their ten percent tithe."

"Ten percent, huh?"

"Are you going to keep throwing it up in my face?" Junior protested from across the room. "I've always paid my ten percent. At least most of the time."

"It's what the good word says. Most members of the congregation don't pay the full tithe." He picked up the Bible next to the collection plate and walked back into his office. He held onto the money in one hand and the Bible in the other. "If you will excuse me, I have to go write next week's sermon. Thank you for your help. You have no idea what a ray of light it was to see you yesterday and this morning."

"Thank you," I said. "Your sermon was lovely, and I was happy to see the old photo of you and Granny and . . ." I tapped my temple before I took the picture out of my pocket. "Granny, you and Mamie Sue Preston."

Pastor Brown's eyes drew together in an agonized expression. I held the picture up so he could get a good, long look and I could get a read on his face. There was definitely surprise and shock running throughout his body.

"Pastor, are you okay?" I asked.

"Fine. Fine." He rocked back and forth. He put the ledger and the Bible, along with the money, back on the table. "I had no idea you knew Mamie Sue Preston."

"Oh, she and Granny were good friends." I for sure was going to get struck by lightning.

"They were?" He looked shocked. "It wasn't the same after Mamie Sue moved away, and then came back."

"Mamie Sue moved away from Sleepy Hollow?" This was news to me.

"Right after we graduated from high school."

He paused and took the picture out of my hands. "As a matter of fact, a couple weeks after this photo was taken, I went off to seminary school. I came home about a month into school to visit, and Mamie Sue had gone. Zula Fae told me she went to visit Mamie and she was gone. Disappeared."

"Really?" I asked. "Disappeared?"

"It wasn't until years later, after I had taken over as the pastor here at Sleepy Hollow Baptist, when Mamie showed up in the front pew, looking just like the teenage girl she'd always been." He laughed. "She was the envy of all the women in the Auxiliary. She had on a big hat and fancy clothes."

"I bet." I could only imagine what Ruthie Sue Payne and Granny thought when they saw Mamie Sue strutting down the aisle at the Sunday service. "Where was she all those years?"

"I don't know. We never really talked after she moved back." He handed the photo back to me. "She became sort of a recluse. She had her family's wealth and she had the big house in the new Triple Thorn subdivision. She had everything she needed. But God . . ." He pointed upward. "She came to church every single Sunday. I tried to reach out to her, but she kept everyone at arm's length."

"Did she?" Then it would make sense to leave the millions. "Did she tithe her ten percent?"

"I have no idea what kind of money she had inherited from her family's coal mine shutting down in Eastern Kentucky, but she did make up for years of not being part of the congregation," he said.

"Did she have any family?" I knew Fluggie Callahan had told me Mamie didn't.

Which reminded me, I hadn't heard from Fluggie in a couple of days. I was going to have to stop by the old mill and see if she'd uncovered any more details about DD LLC.

"None." He shook his head. "Her momma and daddy were both the only children in their families. She was the only child between them. Plus she never got married. Say, why all the interest in Mamie Sue Preston?"

"I had seen her headstone from afar when I was finishing up Cephus Hardy's funeral. I found it interesting, that's all." I sucked in a deep breath and tucked a piece of hair behind my ear. "I asked Granny about her, and she told me she was an old friend."

"Really?" Pastor Brown asked. "I'm glad to see Zula Fae forgiving Mamie."

"What do you mean?" I asked.

"You know that Granny of yours can be a grudge holder. I thought she was going to rip Mamie's fancy hat off during the singing of 'Amazing Grace' when someone told her Mamie had switched her funeral arrangements to Burns." He shook his head. "It wasn't one of Zula Fae's finest moments."

"I'd say not," I agreed.

"I'm just glad to see Zula is forgiving in her older years. We aren't getting any younger. Thankfully, our Lord doesn't hold grudges." He picked the ledger and the money back up. "I really have to get going. Next week's sermon isn't going to write itself. Don't forget about the spaghetti dinner."

"See you Wednesday." I closed my eyes and tried to swallow the lump in my throat. I held onto the table just in case the big guy in the sky struck me dead. I wasn't planning on going to the spaghetti dinner or next week's service, but I wasn't telling Pastor Brown.

I got up and left out the front door of the church. I couldn't stop smiling.

I guess a man of the cloth wasn't too good for a little gossip.

I looked up to the heavens and whispered, "Thank you."

Chapter 21

The chirping noise coming from my back pocket wasn't my normal text tone. I had forgotten Jack Henry had given me the new phone and I hadn't yet figured out the new settings.

It was a text from Charlotte Rae. A girl from Dusting Dixies was at Eternal Slumber to see me. She'd followed it up with an emoji of a grumpy face.

"Bring it on Monday." I did a little skip down the street back toward the funeral home.

"Wait." Junior planted himself in front of me.

Even though he was a ghost and I knew I could blow right through him, it still creeped me out, so I giddy-upped on around him.

"Aren't you going to go and try to figure out my bank account or something?" he asked.

"If there is something you need to tell me, then tell me," I encouraged him.

"That's the problem." The wrinkles around his eyes deepened.

We stopped. He fanned the smoke that was coming from his toupee away from his face.

"What's the problem?" I coughed the words in my hand like I was choking, just in case someone saw me talking to myself. The last thing I needed was a visit from Doc Clyde, and the last thing Granny needed was someone telling her I was crazy. She was already going nuts trying to figure out who was planting all these stolen items in her Inn.

"I see things I think you need to know about. I have no idea what they mean to me and my murder. I only know I got a feeling you need to check them out." His tone rang out with desperation. "I really want to go to the other side. Mamie Sue might be having a good time in this Between area, but not me. No sir-ree am I liking this at all."

"What exactly do you want me to look into?" I needed something to go on. Some sort of path, since I hadn't even looked into his murder.

"I have stolen a pie. I have stolen money from the Lord. I needed you to see my tithe, and I need you to investigate that."

"You mean to tell me you are stealing all of this

stuff and pinning it on Granny?" I couldn't believe I had to help a thief in the afterlife.

"I needed your attention." He protested like what he had done was a-okay. "You pay a lot of attention to Zula."

"You have my attention now." I stopped right in front of Pose and Relax.

"Are you okay, Emma Lee?" John Howard was on the sidewalk with a hammer in his hand.

"Emma, God I'm so glad to see you." Hettie Bell pulled me into the yoga studio and John Howard followed. Junior did not follow, he was nowhere to be seen. "I saw John Howard working so hard on your flower bed, and I asked him for a tiny favor." She held her finger and thumb together with a little distance between them. "I wanted to see if he could nail down the squeaky board. But when I walk all over the floor, it doesn't squeak. Can you remember where it was?"

I walked on the floor a couple of times, but nothing happened.

"It seems I fixed it doing my fake yoga." I tapped her on the back. "Gotta go. I've got a date with a cleaning lady for Eternal Slumber," I said.

I also had a date with Junior Mullins at his place in the home of the near dead. I left that little tidbit out.

"Dang." Hettie Bell scratched her head. "Are you sure you can't remember?"

"Nope." I stepped back outside and nearly ran right over Mable Claire, who was walking down the sidewalk.

"You have got to watch where you are going." Mable Claire jumped out of the way.

"Just the person I wanted to see." I noticed the Dusting Dixies van in the driveway of Eternal Slumber over Mable Claire's shoulder. "How is Beulah?" I asked.

"I don't know. I haven't seen her." Mable Claire adjusted the yoga mat under her arm.

"You didn't go see her this morning?" It seemed odd, since they were thicker than thieves. More important, I wanted the answer to why she couldn't volunteer to count the church offering.

"No."

"Oh, I volunteered to count the church collection, since you couldn't be there." I shook my head. "I couldn't believe all the cash people give to the church."

"Money? I thought it was missing." She jammed the mat even further under her arm.

"No." I couldn't help but notice how much she fidgeted.

"Oh dear." She bit her lip. "I have to go."

"Is there something you need to tell me?" I called after her.

She didn't answer. She stuck her hand in the air, waving me off, and waddled down the street.

Mable Claire's behavior was odd. She knew something, but what?

The blue Dusting Dixies van sat in the driveway of Eternal Slumber. On the side of the van, there was a big white dandelion being held by a fairy with wings. The fairy was carefully blowing the dandelion. The little white seeds were in the shape of a fluffy duster. It was cute. Killer cute?

"I'm so sorry I'm running late." I walked in and noticed it wasn't Dixie Dunn, who I expected. "Oh."

"Hi, Dixie sent me." Tinsie smiled. "She didn't like the idea of a funeral home with the dead and all. Plus none of the other girls wanted to do it, so she just sent me."

She stood with a blue apron tied neatly around her waist. Her hair was pulled up in the plume of black I had originally seen when she'd opened the door to Mamie Sue's mansion.

Tinsie was tiny, like her voice. She had a clipboard and pen in hand. There was something written on the paper that was clipped on the clipboard.

"I went through some of the checklist while I was waiting for you." She turned the clipboard around so fast, I didn't see a thing. "Things like curtain cleaning." She leaned in and covered her mouth with the back of the clipboard. She whispered, "The other girl says it's important."

"Yeah." I rolled my eyes, knowing she was talking about Charlotte Rae. "I'm sorry I had no idea we had an appointment."

"Oh." Tinsie's face reddened. "I thought we said today before you got the boot from Ms. Bellefry's house."

"No biggie." I shrugged.

That night and the moment with Beulah Paige were a little blurry, especially since Beulah had blamed me for her untimely illness.

"Where do you want to start?" I asked.

I was disappointed that Dixie wasn't the one who showed up. It was Dixie I had the questions for.

"Like I said." She pushed her fingers in her messy bird's nest, adjusting what was falling down. "I had already gotten a start. The estimate will not include when there is a dead body lying in one of those rooms." She did a shimmy shake. "Eww. The thought."

"Really? They are dead." I laughed and ignored

Mamie Sue, who had decided to show up. "At least their living form is dead."

"What does that mean?" Suddenly Tinsie's face went grim.

"Oh, a little undertaker humor never hurt anyone." I gave a wry smile, but she wasn't budging.

"I think we should get started." She held the clipboard close to her chest. "I'm not feeling the humor in this job. And it's going to cost you more, since it's . . ."

"Got all sorts of dead people in the freezer?" I laughed. Her expression grew still. "I'm joking. I understand. I got the cold shoulder all my life when I asked people to come over."

"You mean you live here?" she asked. Her brows arched.

"All my life." I pointed down the hallway. "Back there was where I grew up with my family. Then my sister and I took over, and we did an entire remodel, leaving me a little efficiency in the back."

"It doesn't bother you when you have dead people up here?" She nodded toward one of the viewing rooms.

"Not a bit." I kept my jokes to myself. "Enough about me. You are going to be the one who cleans?"

"Unfortunately I'm all you got." She peeked

inside the viewing room and stepped inside. I believe she was looking to see if any clients were laid out.

Sadly, business wasn't booming.

"Emma Lee!" Charlotte Rae bounded down the hall. Her heels clicked with rage. "All the Auxiliary women have decided to cancel their pre-need arrangements because of Beulah Paige Bellefry's fight with you." She stopped at the entryway of the viewing room. She didn't care Tinsie was there; she was going to tear into me. "Do you want to tell me all about it?"

"Well," Tinsie spoke up. "Emma Lee had diarrhea and used Beulah's personal bathroom in her bedroom. But that's not all."

"I think she was asking me." I scowled at the new cleaning lady. "It wasn't *that* bad."

"Oh, you mean when you tested out all the perfumes and the makeup?" Tinsie asked.

"You did what?" Charlotte Rae's body was shaking with fury. She tapped the toe of her fancy tan heels.

Today she wore a green pantsuit, making her red hair pop around her like she was an angel.

"It is a really good moisturizer," Tinsie said. "You should try it. You look like you care about your looks."

Charlotte Rae straightened her shoulders and flicked her long, curly hair down her back.

"Yes. I'm glad you can tell that *unlike* my sister," her hazel eyes slid toward me, "I like to be presentable, and I feel it's very important for the business we are in. Unfortunately, she is single-handedly killing our business, for a lack of better words."

"I'll just run out to the van and grab you a sample." Tinsie headed toward the front door of the funeral home, leaving me with Charlotte Rae.

When the door clicked closed, I knew I was in trouble.

"How on earth do you think we are going to stay alive with all of your crazy behavior?" Charlotte Rae threw her hands in the air.

"But . . ."

"But nothing! I have a home to take care of. I like to look nice, so I have a clothes budget, and you are dipping into it with every single meddling situation you put us in." She shook her perfectly manicured finger at me. She must've just come from the salon, because they were not her usual shade of color, pink. They were fire red, to match her hair and anger. "This is it. I didn't want to tell you like this, but I'm going to be taking a position with Hardgrove Funeral Homes."

"You are what?" The room had suddenly gotten

chillier than the freezer in the basement. There was a bite in the air. Tinsie walked in and stood quietly behind Charlotte. I wanted to blurt out what Arley had told me about Hardgrove, but my anger stopped me.

Charlotte Rae needed to see the grass wasn't greener on the other side.

"Hardgrove has been pursuing me for a few months." She winked at me. "Years, if you know what I mean. But who's counting?" She had a smug look on her face. "I didn't say anything, because I felt bad for leaving you. But when we had so many cancellations, I realized that I can't keep bailing you out." Her words were cold and exact. "I'm sorry, Emma. But this is all yours. I even had the lawyers draw up the papers to put you in charge of this mess."

"Have you told Granny about this?" I asked.

The whiz of a moped was heard in the distance. It was getting closer and closer. I knew it was Granny.

"I guess you don't have to answer that." I glared at Charlotte Rae.

We had always had our differences, but we were family, in a family business. Charlotte didn't see it that way. She never had. She'd always seen it as an income.

"I told Hardgrove I could start immediately." Charlotte's lids lowered.

The front door of the funeral home slammed shut; Granny stomped in.

"What the hell do you think you are doing?" Granny's eyes bugged through the magnified lenses of her aviator glasses, and her hair stuck out from underneath the tight helmet. "Charlotte Rae, you get right back in that office and do your job. The job I left in your hands." She turned to me. "And you, you get in your office and stay in your office. Not run all over town volunteering for the church, going to church, and showing up at Auxiliary meetings." She glared at Tinsie. "You clean this place up, and I mean clean it up!"

Tinsie opened her mouth. Granny put her whole hand out in front of Tinsie to shut her up.

"Granny, I'm sorry." Charlotte Rae lifted her chin, not looking directly at Granny. She lowered her eyes. "I've already taken the job, and I'm going to train tomorrow."

"Tomorrow?" Granny shrilled, huffing and puffing out of her nose. "Wait until your momma and daddy hear you jumped ship! Going over to those no-good Hardgroves."

I thought Granny was going to blow, just like a pressure cooker.

On that note, Tinsie's mouth shut. She pinched her lips together and darted outside. We heard the sound of the Dusting Dixies van doors slamming.

Charlotte Rae tugged on the edges of her fancy green suit coat. "I'm not going to be able to stay at this circus you want to call a funeral home. We are the joke of this and every town around us. Do Momma and Daddy know what you've done?" Charlotte warned Granny.

I was sure the floor shook from underneath me from Granny's anger spewing out of her body.

"I will not lose my license because of her!" Charlotte Rae jabbed her finger at me.

"Me?" I took a small offense at her words.

"Yes." Fire came out of Charlotte Rae's eyes. "You! In one year you have single-handedly torn down a family business that took years to create!"

"Now, that is not fair," I protested. "You could've left your little throne in there and hit the pavement like me."

"You need to be locked up." She did the crazy sign around her ear. "You are crazy! Crazy!"

"Wait just a minute." Granny stopped Charlotte from storming off. "Emma Lee is not crazy. She is doing the best she can, but this is a joint venture I felt the both of you could do together."

Tinsie came back in with her head down and her

hands filled with a bucket of cleaning supplies. She took out the duster and sprayed something on it before she started going over the curtains.

"I can't do it anymore, Granny." Charlotte Rae's voice softened. "I love you. I do, and when I told Mom and Dad about me leaving, I thought Dad was going to have a heart attack, just like the one Emma Lee gave poor Beulah Paige."

"I didn't give anyone a heart attack. Besides," I grumbled, "Beulah Paige is only in her forties."

"Granny." Charlotte Rae wouldn't even look at me. "I'm sorry. I want better for myself."

"Better for yourself is being with your family."

"I'm sorry," Charlotte Rae said again. Then she turned on her fancy shoes and made her way back to her office. "I'll gather my things. Emma Lee knows everything I do and can kill the rest of Eternal Slumber."

"Nice choice of words." Tears stained the lids of my eyes.

"I've got your cream." Tinsie spoke up like she didn't witness the entire crumbling of Eternal Slumber.

She followed Charlotte Rae back to her office.

"Now what?" Granny took a deep breath. "When did Charlotte Rae get above her raisin'?"

"I have an idea." I ran my hand down her arm.

"I have to head over to Happy Times Retirement Community to finish up some business with Junior Mullins's estate. I can put together a package for the residents there."

"Sort of like a half-off package?" Granny tapped her temple.

"Yeah. Something like that," I lied. I had no idea what I was going to offer them, but I did know I was going to save Eternal Slumber.

"I'm going to have to ask Hettie Bell to work at the Inn full-time until we can figure this out." Granny looked out the window of the viewing room. "She's not doing so good anyway. I bet she could use the extra cash." She reached out and squeezed my hand. "I'll take care of all the financial business here. You go and drum up some business."

With a thin smile across my face and worry in my eyes, I nodded. Granny wasted no time. She rushed out of the funeral home, and I watched through the windows as she ran next door to Pose and Relax. It wasn't like I had to have Granny do the financial part, it was the fact I needed support. It wasn't like Charlotte Rae ever gave me support, but it was nice knowing Charlotte was here. At least, I thought she was.

Chapter 22

Eternal Slumber was in dire financial straits, and I had to do something about it.

I still had the murders of Mamie Sue Preston and Junior Mullins weighing on me, and I wasn't getting anywhere fast.

Junior Mullins's home of the near dead was a perfect place to drum up business for Eternal Slumber.

"What are you doing?" Mamie Sue asked from the passenger side of the hearse. "This is not getting me to the other side."

"No, but it is going to help me save my business." I glared at her. "Unfortunately I don't get paid to get you to the other side. I need money to save the funeral home, and the only way to save it is to get some business."

"I told you I would pay you." Mamie tapped her cane on the dash of the hearse.

"In what? Ghost money?" I asked sarcastically.

"I've got money. I'll let you know where to find it once you get the job done." Mamie adjusted the pillbox hat on top of her head. "Trust me. You'll want it."

"Yeah," I laughed and headed the hearse down the curvy road where Happy Times was located. "Monopoly money isn't going to keep the funeral home floating."

There wasn't time to worry about trying to get more clues for Mamie Sue and Junior. I'd have to leave it up to Fluggie Callahan. I reached for my new phone and dialed.

"Hey, Fluggie," I left a message when her answering machine came on. "It's Emma Lee. I haven't heard from you. I need to know if you've figured anything out about the million Mamie left to the church and Dixie Dunn's hand in Mamie Sue's estate. I'm going to be working on saving my funeral home. Long story." I sucked in a deep breath and turned the hearse into the parking lot of Happy Times. "Call me."

I parked in one of the visitor parking spots up

front, right next to a Dusting Dixies fairy van. How many of these vans did they have? And why was I suddenly seeing them all over Sleepy Hollow?

"Nice." I looked around at the scenic backdrop. It wouldn't be bad to spend the last days of your life looking out over the beautiful, mountainous landscape Sleepy Hollow had to offer. It was one of the main draws for visitors to the community. The Sleepy Hollow Inn kept Granny busy, because tourists loved to hike the gorges and caves surrounding our little paradise. The views at Happy Times didn't disappoint.

I opened the glove box and grabbed a handful of Eternal Slumber brochures. The idea of going in the nursing home gave me more of the creeps than being around the dead and their corpses. Just the fact they were on the verge of death and the next minute they were dead gave me the heebie-jeebies. Going in here to drum up business was an O'Dell Burns tactic, not mine.

"Well," I took a deep breath. "O'Dell is no longer in charge. Neither is Charlotte." I swept the large glass door open and said, "There's a new sheriff in town."

"What?" A hunchbacked old lady sitting in a wheelchair used her heels to roll over to me. "That hot hunk Jack Henry Ross is no longer sheriff?"

"Yes, ma'am."

I felt sorry for her. Was this how the rest of her life was going to play out? Stuck in the wheelchair, never to go outside these institutional pale yellow walls?

"Shoo." Her lips pursed. "You nearly put one of my feet in the grave coming in here saying there's a new sheriff in town."

I laughed. I hated to inform her, but one of her feet was already dangling in the grave.

"What's this about a new sheriff?" A little old man with paper-thin hair and large hearing aids sticking out of both ears made his way over to us. His walker creaked with each step.

He obviously didn't hear the noise, or surely he would have had it oiled up.

"Nothing, Sunny." The old lady snorted. "You go mind your own business."

"Whatever, Imogene." Sunny's nose curled.

"He can't hear." She lifted her head and looked at me. "Just nosy. What's in your hand?"

Talk about nosy.

"My name is Emma Lee Raines, and I own Eternal Slumber." I kind of felt good not saying I co-owned it with my sister. "And we are featuring a special. If you sign up today for pre-need arrangements, you get half off the cemetery stone."

"Good marketing coming here," Imogene quipped. "Sunny! This here is Emma Lee, and she wants to bury you!" she yelled. "Gonna give you a deal if you die today!"

"Pish posh!" Sunny threw his hands in the air and quickly grabbed the sides of the walker when he tipped backward.

"Can I help you?" A young girl in blue scrubs greeted me. She eyed Imogene and Sunny. "Don't mind those two. They are always at each other . . . in good fun." She winked. "They might be old, but they still flirt." She clapped her hands in front of her. "How can I help you?"

"I wanted to talk to the manager or someone who would let me . . ." I had to pick my words wisely. "Um . . . let me hold a funeral fair."

"Funeral fair?" Her brows formed a V.

"I own Eternal Slumber in town, and we know your residents are on a fixed income. It really isn't fair that when the time comes, we leave all our arrangements to our families to be made. Leaving them with a large debt to the funeral homes." I gave her a brochure. "My sister—" *Ahem*, I cleared my throat. I was going to have to change my whole pitch now that Charlotte Rae was out of the picture. "I believe that when a loved one passes, it's much easier on the family financially and emotionally if the deceased has already made all the decisions on the arrangements. Not leaving it up to the family. That creates a lot of stress."

"I see." She sucked in her lower lip. Her eyes narrowed. "Do you think our elders can't afford arrangements?"

"I'm not sure what they can afford." I wasn't sure what she was asking me. "I was just trying to help out."

"And you thought coming here would be a great idea since we look like we are almost six feet under, like your clients?" The woman was offended. It was apparent on her face.

"I'm sorry if I came across wrong, but that was not my intention at all." I opened up the brochure to the middle, where there was a picture of Charlotte Rae visiting with a family making pre-need arrangements. "Here are the statistics of stress when a loved one dies with no pre-need arrangements, compared to the stress of a family who did have arrangements."

"I'm joking." The woman laughed along with Sunny and Imogene. "Of course you can come in here and talk to our residents. Only you should know this is a high-end retirement community. Not nearly ready for them to meet their maker."

"I might look almost dead." Imogene poked her

chest. "The ticker is good. I do have some needs made with Burns, but I'd be willing to change for the right price."

"Hmm . . ." I was going to play the hot hunk card. "What if I get Sheriff Jack Henry Ross to come give you a ride in his cruiser?"

"Where do I sign?" Imogene rubbed her wrinkly hands together.

The manager let me set up shop in the room where the residents held their poker tournaments on Tuesday and Thursday nights. There was an on-site chef, on-site lap pool—I'd never seen so many old men in Speedos—and an on-site physical fitness room.

Hettie Bell was missing out in the yoga department. This was for sure her target range.

The entire joint was way nicer than my efficiency. I was sure it cost a pretty penny to stay here, and Junior Mullins apparently lived here for years.

After I signed up three new clients, the word spread about the special, and I had a line of takers.

Suddenly I found Dixie Dunn standing over me with her dusting wand. "It looks like you are drumming up business." She was going to town on the chair rail.

"Hi, Dixie." I watched her with a curious eye.

"Thank you for sending Tinsie over to the funeral home this morning. I truly appreciate it."

"Glad to. I hope it worked out." Her hand went back and forth in a rapid motion, dusting anything standing still.

"I'm shocked to see you here," I made the observation. "I thought you said you worked for Beulah Paige Bellefry full-time."

"I did before her seeing you put her in the hospital," she whispered between her gritted teeth. "They aren't even sure if she's going to make it. You cost me a job. A big job. Now I have to come here and drum up business with all of these people."

"Oh." I looked down, not sure what to say.

"Kind of like what you are doing since your sister quit on you." Her words stung.

In fact, her words hurt. I could only imagine what the rest of the town was going to say when they found out Charlotte Rae had left Eternal Slumber. According to Charlotte Rae, the entire town thought I still had the Funeral Trauma, and they only stuck around because of her. I was quickly going to change that. I glanced down at the fifty applications.

"Oh, Dixie." Mamie Sue stood next to us. "If only you would have taken my advice and done something with the money for your creams."

"What about your facial creams?"

"What 'bout them?" Her eyes held mine.

"Why don't you do something with that? I mean, you do still have Mamie Sue's business at her estate, and I'm sure it pays you handsomely."

"I don't take handouts from no one. My mom didn't, and I don't." She pointed the dusty wand at me and shook the dust out all over my new contracts. "You got that?"

Whether I got it or not, she shuffled out of the room in a rage. I understood her being mad about the job at Beulah's being on hold, but what she'd said about being hired by the residents here struck a chord with me.

The manager walked past.

"Excuse me." I put my hand out to stop her. "Did you say everyone here pays for what they need?"

"Yes," she confirmed.

"What about cleaning service?" I asked.

"For the entire facility we hired Dusting Dixies, but each individual room is either done by themselves or they can hire out privately. Why? Don't tell me you have a cleaning service too?"

"I just buried Junior Mullins. I did pick him up here, and I wondered if he had a cleaning service." I tried not to be too obvious.

"I'm sorry, Ms. Raines." She smiled sweetly and said, "We aren't allowed to give out client information. It would go against the HIPAA law. I'm sure you would understand."

"Of course." I smiled.

Of course I understood. It didn't mean I accepted it. No way in hell did I accept it.

If Dusting Dixies was Junior's cleaning service, and Dixie was Mamie's cleaning lady, and Beulah's . . .

"Oh my God!" I jumped up, with a line of clients ready to sign up. I gathered my belongings. "I'll be back later. I have to go somewhere."

"Wait, I didn't get a chance to sign up!" Sunny yelled over the crowd. "And I want half off my stone!"

"Fine." I got close to Sunny because I wanted him to hear me loud and clear the first time. "I'll give you an entire package for free if you tell me all you know about Junior Mullins."

Beulah was in the hospital. There was nothing I could do about her situation. She could wait a little bit longer. I needed to get into Junior Mullins's apartment. Fast.

"You've got you a deal." His lips puckered around his gummy smile. "I've been wanting to tattle on that little poker cheater for a long time."

"Great." I smiled and took him by the elbow. He held on to his walker. "Why don't we go down to the cafeteria and let me buy you a coffee."

"One of them fancy kind with chocolate and whipped cream?" he asked.

"Anything you want." There was something in my soul telling me there was more to Junior Mullins's death than just old age. Dixie Dunn had had a hand in it, but how?

Dixie Dunn seemed to have a little hand in everything around Sleepy Hollow and its residents, who were dropping like flies.

Chapter 23

The lattes in the Happy Times cafeteria would really give Cheryl Lynne Doyle and Higher Grounds Café a run for her money. I watched Sunny lick, slurp and sip his drink until he was ready to talk.

"How well did you know Junior Mullins?" I asked as he licked the whipped cream on top.

I glanced around the cafeteria-styled room. Underneath awnings attached to the wall were different stations for different appetites—Italian, Thai, Chinese, American, vegan. Anything any of them wanted was right there for their tasting palates. There was even the little café stand where we had gotten our fancy coffees.

"Know me?" Junior bounced up and down, creating smoke rings all over the room. "He tried to take me to the cleaners every week during our poker tournament."

There was the money thing again. It seemed Junior had had money and everyone knew but me.

"He was an old coot." Sunny's mouth dipped. "Though I never figured he was going to kick the bucket." He elbowed me. "You know, eeck." He drew his finger across his neck.

"Are you telling me he was murdered?" I found it odd he would choose the cutting gesture.

"Murdered?" He drew back. "Nah. I'm just saying he didn't look good. Sorta bad."

"I was damn fine!" Junior spat at the ground.

"What do you mean by 'sort of'?" I cautiously asked, well aware it must be time for afternoon snack.

The lunchroom-style tables were filling up with many residents having a cup of coffee and afternoon treat.

"A couple weeks ago, he started complaining of headaches. I thought it was because I was beating the pants off him." Sunny smacked his leg in delight, and then grew serious. "For the next few days, he started to get pale. Even his eczema grayed." He shook his head. A sadness bore deep in his eyes, like he could see that the ghost of Junior Mullins was right in front of him. "He said he couldn't shake the headache and felt tired. I told him to go to the doctor, but he said it had to be his allergies acting up."

"Eczema?" I asked.

"Hell, all us old people have skin conditions." Sunny raised up the sleeve of his plaid shirt and showed me some flaky skin that would probably go away with a little bit of lotion.

"Next thing I knew, Junior didn't show up to play poker. I went up to check on him." He patted his walker next to him. "It takes me a while to get up there, but when I got there," he gulped, "he didn't answer. The door was cracked, and I pushed it open to find him lying on the floor. Dead."

"His door was open?" I asked. He nodded. "Was his door always open?"

"No. We all keep our doors locked. We have our own keys." He patted his pants pocket, and the keys in them jingled.

"Did you tell the police all of this?" I found it strange how the door was open and nothing was investigated.

"I told them I found him dead." He didn't take his eyes off his drink. "The poor sheriff had to put up with all these old hens pecking around him like they was cougars."

"Did you tell him the door was open?" Jack Henry would have thought it was strange, just like I did.

"No. The way I figured it was he was coming downstairs to play poker and he had a heart attack just like the coroner said." He picked up his cup. "I'm gonna drink this now."

"One more question." I held a finger up. "What was Junior's room number?"

"Fourth floor, number twelve." Sunny had a cute whipped cream mustache on his upper lip. I handed him a napkin. In the corner of my eye, I could see Imogene and a few of her woman friends making their way over.

"Number twelve." I made a mental note. "Looks like you've got company, Casanova." I winked and greeted the women before I excused myself.

The halls of Happy Times smelled like mothballs. I had always heard old people loved to put mothballs all over, and now I knew it. Thank God Granny thought she was not old, because I could hardly take the smell. I found the elevator at the end of the hallway waiting for a passenger. I got in and punched the fourth floor. I took the downtime and ride up to text Fluggie.

Something strange. Dixie Dunn is associated with a lot of rich people. She has cleaned for a few. I noticed she has new vans for her cleaning crew. Somehow Mamie's death, Junior Mullins's death, and Beulah Paige Bellefry's illness have to be related. Beulah Paige is a local who suddenly took ill. Where are you? Call me.

I hit send right as the doors slid open. I looked down the hall before I stepped out. No one was around. It was time to see what was in Junior's apartment that might tie Dixie Dunn to him.

The right side of the hallway was odd-numbered apartments, and the left side was even. I didn't bother counting my way down, I just looked for the number as quickly as possible.

"Twelve. One. Two." I tapped the gold numbers nailed to the door. I grabbed the handle and turned, but the door was locked.

"What's going on?" Dixie Dunn asked from the next apartment over. She walked out of the door and put her cleaning pail on the ground in the hallway.

"I was . . ." I paused. "I needed to collect the paperwork from Junior Mullins for his final burial."

"Maybe you need to ask the manager to let you in." She grabbed an aerosol can from her bucket and disappeared back into the apartment she was cleaning. "I can't stand here dillydallying. As it is, I'm going to be here all day."

A set of keys dangling from the wire handle of the cleaning bucket caught my eye. Without thinking, I grabbed them. Each one had a sticker with a number. The first number had to be the floor, then there was a dash, and the next set of numbers.

"Four dash twelve." My eyes lit up when I found Junior's key. I stuck it in the keyhole and turned, opening the door.

I put the keys back where I found them and ran into Junior's apartment. Quietly I closed the door behind me and locked it, just in case she tried to open it to see if I'd made it in.

A shadow of something or someone caught my eye, and I jumped around. No one was there. The place was a one-room apartment that was broken up into sections. He had a queen bed with two side tables. Each with a lamp. Very tidy. His kitchenette was just as clean as the rest of his apartment. Every cabinet was stocked nice and neat with dishes, cups, and glasses. The inside of his microwave was even shiny clean. Not a speck of dried-on splattered food anywhere.

The room off the kitchen was his bathroom. There were a few creams with prescriptions on them for his eczema. I opened the mirrored cabinet on the wall.

"What do we have here?" I picked up a jar of the moisturizer Dixie Dunn had given me.

On the top, written in Sharpie marker, were instructions for Junior on how to apply the cream to the affected area three times a day for two weeks. Two weeks?

Sunny's words rang out in my head about how Junior had complained of a headache a couple weeks ago that had progressively gotten worse.

I reread the label of the moisturizer. My heart sank. Was Dixie Dunn somehow getting these elderly people to put her in their will and then poisoning them through moisturizer?

"No." I pondered the possibilities.

"That's my good cream." Junior appeared next to me when I shut the door "It did good on my skin."

"I'm not sure Dixie Dunn did you one bit of good." I held the jar in my hand. "Did you have Dusting Dixies clean your apartment?"

"I did. Fine job too." He looked out the door of the bathroom. "Cleaning fool. When I had to cancel because I had a doctor's appointment, she asked me what for and I told her I had bad itchy eczema. Other than that, I was pretty healthy."

"Did you happen to change your will over the past few weeks?" I asked.

"How did you know?" He looked at me with an open mouth.

"Who changed your will?" I asked.

"Some guy came here." He thought about it for a minute. "Strange name."

"Emmitt Moss?" I asked.

"Hot dang." He smacked his leg and did a jig. "That's his name. That eczema cream fixed me up good. The cleaner said she didn't have enough money to get the cream into stores. I gave her a few thousand dollars to get some marketing help and even decided to give her a couple million in my will."

"Couple million?" My eyes bolted open. "How in the hell did she get you to give her money in your will?"

"I can't take it with me up there. And she wasn't getting it until I was dead. She kept me company. I told you," he rolled up his sleeve again, "she fixed me up good."

"She sure did fix you up good. Fixed you dead," I said matter-of-factly.

Chapter 24

"Fluggie, where are you?" I said into her answering machine. "You better be knee deep in research, because I have found out some information you aren't going to believe. I've got to stop by the funeral home and then by Beulah Paige's hospital bed to see if my hunch is right. I'll be by if I don't hear from you first."

With Junior's jar of cream in my hand, I wanted to get back to the fancy lab Vernon Baxter had in the basement of Eternal Slumber. A few months back, the city council had voted to equip Vernon Baxter's lab with the latest in DNA and autopsy technology with the incentive money the state had awarded the city. It included poison testing. Vernon would be able to tell me if my hunches were right.

Since Vernon Baxter had retired and moved to Sleepy Hollow, the police had been keeping him busy with autopsies. Plus he did all the embalming for Eternal Slumber.

I pulled into the driveway of the funeral home and was happy to see Charlotte Rae's car wasn't there. I didn't want to spend any energy on her or hearing her yell at me, though she would've been excited to know I had gotten fifty new pre-need arrangements from Happy Times Retirement Community. Now she wouldn't know. Even though Hardgrove was in another city, it was still competition. Charlotte Rae was now on the other team. Blood or not.

I didn't bother using the elevator to go downstairs to where we kept our clients cold and Vernon did his handiwork.

"Hey, Emma Lee." He took his eyes off the microscope and peered at me over the top of his glasses. His steel-blue eyes were striking, like those of old Hollywood film legends Gary Cooper and Peter O'Toole. He ran his hand through his salt-and-pepper hair. "I overheard the ruckus this morning between you and Charlotte Rae. I'm sorry."

"Oh don't worry about her. We are going to be just fine." I handed him the jar of moisturizer. "Listen, I need you to do a side job."

"Oh-kay." Reluctantly he took the jar and looked at it. "Moisturizer?"

"I think there is some sort of poison in the moisturizer." I watched his expression go from shocked to confusion. "I know it sounds weird. But I think there is a serial killer in Sleepy Hollow."

"Serial killer?"

"Serial killer." The sound of those two words made the hairs on my neck stand up. "I think Junior Mullins, along with another resident of Sleepy Hollow, were poisoned to death. And I think she might have struck again with Beulah Paige."

"Did you get clearance from Jack Henry about this?" he asked.

"No. I don't want to say anything until I get these results back." I pushed the button on the elevator. "Let me know what you find out."

"Don't worry. I will." Vernon opened the jar and immediately started to take samples and put them in little test tubes.

There was no time to waste. I needed to get over to the hospital to see what the doctors were saying about Beulah Paige. If my instincts were right, Dixie Dunn had gotten her toe in Beulah's door and was trying to kill her with whatever it was she put in the cream.

I looked in the rearview mirror.

"Shit, shit, shit." I ran my hands down my face. I had slathered that shit all over me last night. But I felt fine. I didn't feel sick. "Shit."

It was time to exercise my job as undertaker. I pulled the hearse right up to the emergency room exit of the hospital. No one would dare put a ticket on the windshield or call a tow truck if they thought some poor, pitiful dead person was being taken to their final resting place.

I shimmied through the sliding-glass doors before they were fully opened. The receptionist pulled her glasses off her face, and they dangled from the long chain down her front. She looked past me and saw the hearse.

"Can you please tell me what room Beulah Paige Bellefry is located in?" I asked.

"She didn't die." The woman typed away on her computer. "Did she?"

"Not that I know of, but I know her, and while I was here doing my job"—I glanced back at the hearse, and then back at her—"I thought I would pay my respects to her after what had happened."

"Yes. She's in ICU north." She pointed down the hall and gave a few directions on how to get there before she sent me on my way.

She had me so turned around, I have no idea how I got there, but I did.

The sign on the entrance read PUSH THE BUTTON TO ENTER. I pushed the button.

"Can I help you?" a woman's voice asked through the intercom.

The last time I did this at Mamie Sue's house, it didn't go so well.

"Yes." I did my best Southern drawl, just like Beulah Paige Bellefry. "My dear aunt has had a spell, and I'm here to pay her a visit. Beulah Paige Bellefry."

"You are her niece?" the woman chirped.

"Yes." My voice dripped of sweetness and lies.

"Room three." The door shot open. I half expected to see the woman behind the mic, but no one was there.

The ICU rooms were around the perimeter of a large desk full of people in scrubs looking at computers or talking amongst one another. None of them paid a bit of attention to me as I ducked in room three, where Beulah Paige Bellefry would've had a heart attack if she'd seen how her lipstick was smeared and dripping down her face.

Not that I really cared, but I took the sponge at the end of the stick thingy and put it in the water next to the bed. I dipped it in and gently rubbed down her face, getting most of the lipstick smear off.

"Well, well." I glanced down at her lifeless body. Tubes coming out every which way. The heart monitor she was hooked up to showed that her heart was beating at a steady pace. "Haven't you gotten yourself in a jam? And it's going to be little ole me who gets you out of it. Again."

Once before, not too long ago, Beulah Paige had been right in the exact same place after being attacked. Of course, they'd thought I had done her in, because we had mixed words right in front of Eternal Slumber. My words might have had "death" and "going to kill you" or "over my dead body" in them. Naturally, someone had overheard and had me pegged as the attacker.

She obviously wasn't too grateful I had saved her life once, because here we were again. Right back where we started a few months back.

"Now." I looked around the room for a report. I had no idea what I would do with it, but maybe something would jump out.

"Good evening." A young gentleman came in. "You must be Ms. Bellefry's niece."

He shoved his hand into mine, giving it a good couple of pumps.

"Was she feeling dizzy, having headaches, or

pains?" He shot questions out to me like firing a semiautomatic. "Vomiting, delirium?"

"I know she had a major headache for a couple days, but since I don't live with her, I'm not sure about the other stuff." I was beginning to believe my own lies.

"All her tests are coming back negative. No heart attack, no stroke." He folded one arm around him and rested his other elbow on it. He wiggled his finger in the air. "You know." He shook his head. "Nah."

"What?" I asked. I needed to know what had him so perplexed.

"If I didn't know better, I'd think she had been poisoned with arsenic." He threw his hands in the air. "The test results will tell us."

"Arsenic?" I whispered.

Going back to mortuary school, I remember them saying something about how arsenic can be disguised in many things and can be absorbed through your skin pores. Even the ones on your face.

"Moisturizer." I smacked my hands together and grabbed the doctor, giving him a big kiss on the cheek. "Thank you, Doctor!"

I scrammed out of the ICU and took the stairs down the four flights as fast as I could.

"Thanks!" I yelled to the receptionist in the emergency room as I flew by her desk.

"Wait!" she screamed. "Did you forget a body?"

"Oh." I stopped in front of the sliding doors and waited for them to open. "The damnedest thing. He started breathing as soon as I put my hand on him to take him to the freezer."

The doors opened, letting me escape back into the safety of my hearse. Nervously, I fumbled for my phone. I had to call Jack Henry and tell him what I had found out.

Chapter 25

Was there a party and I wasn't invited? I asked myself while I waited for the beep on his answering machine. When it picked up, I said, "I know you are going to be mad at me and I'm apologizing. Or I'll make up for it later. But Dixie Dunn is swindling old rich people out of their money and getting them to change their wills, leaving her millions in cash. She is killing them by having them use this moisturizer cream laced with arsenic." I sucked in a breath before I continued. "The moisturizer is nice. But Beulah." I tapped the wheel. "Beulah has arsenic poisoning. I took her jar of cream. Details later, but that's what is wrong with her. I gave Vernon Baxter the jar I had taken from Junior Mullins's apartment in the old folks home. Only it's not an old folks home, and you need to give Imogene a ride." I rambled on. I wasn't sure what to say. "Okay. Fluggie Callahan is probably at the old mill, and she's been helping me. Emmitt Moss is a bad, bad man. Damn!" I screamed when his tape ran out of room.

I had already said enough for him to go and investigate. It took everything in me not to rush over to Mamie Sue's and gather evidence that might be there. *Might* was the operative word. Jack Henry had warned me not to get involved. It was high time I listened to him. I was confident he would get my message and follow up on the leads. He would call me and let me know what was going on.

Fluggie still hadn't called me back or texted me. I could picture her on the phone getting all sorts of good information. In order to keep me out of trouble but not fully out of the investigation, I decided to head out to the old mill and see what she had uncovered. If she wasn't there, I could wait until I heard from Jack Henry.

As soon as I turned on the old country road, my thoughts did change gears to Jo Francis Ross and Jack Henry. I had been able to stick the entire situation in the back of my head. Mamie Sue's and Junior's deaths helped keep the heartache at bay. The idea of Jack Henry moving hours and a state away left a heavy feeling in my stomach. It wasn't what I wanted. It had always been what he wanted. I will never forget a single detail of the most embarrassing night of my life. High school and the ill-fated game of spin the bottle.

Jack Henry probably didn't remember how he'd talked about his future and how he dreamed of being an FBI agent. He said he was going to make it happen, even if he had to move up in ranks. That was right before the bottle had landed on us to kiss and he'd run off. No one wanted to kiss the creepy funeral-home girl.

I let out a heavy sigh, putting the bad memory back in the depths of my brain. Fluggie's old junker station wagon was parked right next to the old mill.

The door of the old mill was locked. I tugged harder. The old mill door was never locked, even before Fluggie moved her office back in there after being gone for a brief absence. I walked over to the window and used my hand to wipe a circle in the dust and filth. Using my hands, I cupped them over my eyes and pressed my nose up against the glass. My eyes shifted left and right before they zeroed in on a pair of feet sticking out from behind Fluggie's desk. I pulled back. Blinked my eyes to make sure I was seeing what I thought I had seen.

I stuck my face up against the window for the second time, immediately feeling sick when the feet were still there.

I ran back to the door.

"Fluggie! Fluggie!" I beat my palms up against the door. I was hoping she was diabetic and was in need of some sugar, but my gut told me Dixie Dunn had gotten wind of Fluggie's snooping around and had done something to her.

"Fluggie!" I grabbed the handle and violently shook my body back and forth, trying to force it open, to no avail. "Damn."

I went back to the window. I took my shoe off my foot and began to beat the windowpanes. Thank God the Hardys, who owned the old mill, didn't replace the old windows when they did the remodel after the explosion. The windows were paper thin, making this one easy to bust.

I made sure the shards of glass weren't going to jab me when I slipped through the window and rushed to Fluggie's side.

"Oh no, oh no," I cried, rolling her over.

There was a pool of blood on the floor, and her hair was matted to her head from the blood.

I put my finger on her neck to see if I could get a

pulse. When I didn't feel anything, I flung my ear down on her chest. Nothing.

I moved down to her wrist. There was a faint pulse.

"Oh, God. Oh God!" I wasn't much of a religious person, but I could sure use some help right now. "I'll volunteer! Anything!"

I grabbed my phone out of my pocket and frantically dialed 911. My fingers shook trying to punch each number.

"Nine." I took a deep breath, trying to focus my eyes. I continued, "One, one." Fluggie was on borrowed time, and there was no time to call Jack Henry.

"I need an ambulance at the old mill!" I screamed through the phone when I heard the dispatcher answer. "Head injury, barely breathing, blood everywhere! Hurry! Call Sheriff Jack Henry Ross immediately!"

I put the phone back in my pocket; I crawled on my knees up to Fluggie's face and gently placed my bloodstained hands on each side. I bent down and whispered in her ear, "I'm so sorry. Do not die on me," I begged her. "I have to stop Dixie Dunn. The ambulance is on the way. Please, please, please don't die."

There wasn't any more time to be wasted. I

couldn't wait for Jack Henry to go through the clues I had left on his voice mail. I had to stop Dixie Dunn before she killed someone else.

I unlocked the old mill door and ran out of there as fast as I could, wiping my hands down my pants to get off the dripping blood.

Dixie Dunn said she was going to be cleaning apartments at Happy Times all day, which meant I could somehow slip into Mamie Sue's house in Triple Thorn and get the real evidence I needed to prove she was lacing the moisturizer.

I floored the hearse as fast as it could go, hugging the curves of the country road. Triple Thorn was clear across town on a different country road, and I needed all the time I could get.

I thought about Dixie and why she would have killed them. Mamie and Junior had both told me they had offered her money to start her business, but she'd refused. Was Dixie that deranged that she would get pure enjoyment out of the thrill of the kill and getting them to put her in their wills?

I didn't have all the answers, but it was a pretty good start. Mark my words, I would have the answers shortly. My eyes darted between the rearview mirror and the side mirrors as I made sure no one was following me. Mamie Sue's file from Doc Clyde's office slid around the front seat. I reached over and grabbed it. I opened it and tried to drive and read at the same time.

The words on the page jumped out at me. The word SYMPTOMS was printed in black letters at the top of the page. Underneath it were the words *vomiting, diarrhea, dizziness, headaches* . . .

"Headaches." I threw the file down and gripped the wheel while pressing the pedal to the floor. I said, "Mamie Sue had all the symptoms the doctor at the hospital asked me if Beulah had. Mamie Sue was poisoned."

I grasped the armrest of the hearse as I skidded in a tight left into the subdivision. The hearse gained speed, barreling down the street, coming to an abrupt halt when I got to the gate. I didn't dare take any chances of any landscapers seeing me. I pulled the car a few doors down and pulled up into Beulah's driveway. The neighbors were going to go crazy seeing a hearse in her circular drive.

Luckily, the house had only large hedges. Mamie Sue's was the only one with a fortress around it. Good for me that I was a loner as a kid and did a lot of tree climbing and hiking in the woods around the caves. I hoisted myself up and over with a little bit of muscle and landed on my feet like a cat. I waited and listened for sounds before I decided to make my way up to the house.

I checked my phone. There wasn't a call from anyone, and the reception was spotty. I only had one of five bars, which meant no one was going to get hold of me. I just prayed Jack Henry had gotten my messages.

The back door was in my vision, and it was probably the best place to enter. Wrong! As soon as I stepped foot in the door, Dixie Dunn was standing there with a half-eaten bologna sandwich in her mouth.

"Good God, Emma Lee, you scared the bejesus out of me." She choked out a piece of bologna. "Want a fried bologna sandwich?"

"You're joking, right?" I asked cautiously. "I mean, you are standing here without a care in the world as Beulah Paige is dying because you poisoned her?"

"I'm telling you, Dixie would never hurt me." Mamie Sue stomped her cane on the floor.

"And her!" I pointed to the air. Dixie's eyes shifted to the space between us. "You killed Mamie Sue Preston. God rest her soul." I did the sign of the cross. "And you killed Junior Mullins, and I can prove it."

"Is that blood on your hands?" Dixie's frightened eyes looked at my hands, dropped down to the smears on my pants, and back up to my face.

"Yeah, Fluggie Callahan's." I glared at her and put both hands up in the air to give her a good look at what she had done. "Guess what? She's still alive, and you are going to go to jail for trying to kill her."

Dixie leaned on the counter. She patted her hands on the countertop behind her. "I heard you were nuts."

"Tell her, Emma Lee." Junior Mullins stood next to the shadowy figure I had seen a couple times. The figure stepped out into the light. It was a slightly older woman. Not as put-together as Mamie, but not poor. Her blue eyes had dulled, and she had heavy bags under her eyes.

"Pattie?" Mamie Sue put her hand over her mouth before she burst into tears.

"Who's Pattie?" I looked at the ghost.

"Pattie? That was my momma." Dixie pulled a butter knife from behind her back. It dripped with mayonnaise. "How did you know?" She jabbed the dull knife in the air between us. "You stay right there."

She kept the knife in front and used her other hand to grab the phone hanging on the wall.

"You killed your own momma?" I asked in disgust. This was getting way too complicated for me. I pulled my phone out of my pocket. "Go ahead, call Sheriff Ross. He already knows what you have done to Mamie Sue Preston, Junior Mullins and Beulah Paige Bellefry. You can tell him your statement."

"There will be no such activity." Tinsie came around the corner of the kitchen, holding the shiniest 9mm and pointing it toward me. "Okay, Funeral Girl. Momma, take her downstairs and then go upstairs and pack our bags. Emmitt Moss is waiting for us at the airport on his private jet."

"Tinsie! My girl." Junior Mullins stood with a big stupid grin on his face.

"What are you doing?" Dixie shrieked. "Put the gun away. Right this minute."

"Oh my God," I gasped. "You are the killer. Not Dixie."

"Do what I say and no one will die. At least not you, Momma." Shy Tinsie suddenly found her voice.

Dixie ushered me down to the basement, which was just as nice as the first floor.

"What is going on?" Dixie asked, looking between me and her daughter.

"It was all going great, Momma. The moisturizer line was going great. But Pattie." Tinsie's nose curled. "The woman who raised you. She never wanted to see your dreams come true. She wanted you to stay in Lexington. You had to keep working as a maid. She resented you because you got pregnant with me when you were in high school, just like your real mother got knocked up by good ole Pastor Brown."

"Shush your mouth," Dixie scolded her. I put my arm around Dixie. "Are you telling me you killed my momma?"

"Both of them." Tinsie's eyes grew black. "It was working out great until little Miss Death decided to go poking her nose into dead people's business."

"How did you know?" I asked, taking my arm off Dixie. I wanted to get all the answers I could before she killed me.

"Emmitt and I were going to take Momma and this business to the stars." With gun in hand, she swirled her hands in front of her and looked out into the beyond. "It was working out great with Pattie out of the picture."

"We are doing just fine with the cleaning business." Dixie wasted her breath on a daughter who had already admitted to killing two people. Not Junior or Mamie Sue . . . yet.

"Oh, Momma. Look at me! I said look at me!" she screamed at the top of her lungs. "Do I look like I want to clean someone else's shitter the rest of my life?"

Dixie's head fell. Tears rolled down her face.

"What about Mamie Sue Preston?" The words came out of Dixie's mouth as if she were a little child. "Did you kill her?"

"You mean your real mom, who was gracious enough to give you a cleaning job? You weren't good enough to be her daughter, but you were good enough to be her maid?" Tinsie cocked a brow.

"I was young. So was Eugene Brown. It was the summer before he was going to seminary school. Zula Fae had the biggest crush on him." Mamie Sue told the story. "The night before he left, Zula Fae slipped into his room and found me in his arms. After that, he left for seminary. Zula Fae wouldn't talk to me. I left town when I found out I was pregnant. Only I couldn't care for a child." Mamie Sue stood next to Dixie like she could be heard as she bared her heart out. "I made sure I kept in touch with Pattie. I wanted to keep my eye on you. I wanted to make sure you were taken care of. That is why I left you this estate."

"But she left Dixie the estate. Which ultimately meant you," I answered Tinsie.

"I watched my momma scrounge her way to the

top of the chain for this damn moisturizer line. Beg and plead for people to see her. She didn't deserve to wait until the old bag who threw her away like a used cleaning cloth died a natural death." Tinsie snickered. "Emmitt told me how I could get this arsenic pretty easy and slip it in the moisturizer. Then he came up with the brilliant idea to use the cleaning service to get into these rich nursing homes, become friends with them, have them change their wills, and give them a little cream to help out with their eczema."

Tinsie made her way over to the bar. She poured herself a shot of whiskey. Without taking her eyes off me, she slung back the tan liquor, crunching her face up as the elixir slid down her throat.

"Ahh." She shook her head from side to side.

She opened the cabinet.

"Aw man," Junior shuffled his feet. "I thought I had a shot with that little cutie."

"Just like you did Junior Mullins," I stated. "Why Beulah Paige? She wasn't going to leave a cleaning lady any sort of money."

"You have your little snooping to blame for that." Tinsie wiggled the gun to the left, telling me to scoot. She pointed to the floor. I slid down the wall and sat down with my legs bent. "Emmitt told me you came around asking all sorts of questions about Mamie. We knew we had to do away with you."

Tinsie laid the gun on the counter of the bar. She pulled out a couple of vials of a powdery substance and held them under one of the can lights.

"This will kill you in an instant." Her eyes slid from the vial to me. "Just enough of this sprinkled into . . ." She took a jar of moisturizer out of the cabinet, leaving the doors wide open. I could see her little lab of death inside. ". . . this little jar like this." She unscrewed the lid of the jar and sprinkled in a little bit of the powder. Slowly, she mixed the two and continued to tell her sordid tale. "If you apply our wonderful cream to your face as instructed, you will die a slow death. A death that will go undetected unless a little snooping bitch like you gets involved. That is why I have my dearly beloved boyfriend, Emmitt, waiting for me and my momma, along with a case of cash from Junior Mullins's estate and Mamie Sue's."

"I get why you killed your grandmothers, but why Junior?" I had to ask.

Junior sat in the corner with a sad look on his face. He needed answers before he crossed over. Pattie and Mamie Sue stood in the corner, hugging each other.

"Men are men. No matter what age." She

grinned. "I don't mind using my girly figure to get more money from a horny old man like Junior Mullins. I saw his bank statement while I was cleaning. A girl can never have enough cash." She winked, sending shivers up my legs.

"I'm not a horny old man!" He stomped. I noticed the smoke from his toupee was no longer there.

"He would watch me clean his apartment in my skimpy maid outfit." She giggled in a sick, perverted way. "I made sure I bent way over to dust his TV while he was watching." She wiggled her way down into the pose she was talking of. "I gave him my sad story of being born from a whore who could never afford to give me a life outside of cleaning other people's toilets. And I had this wonderful cream that would clear up his eczema. You should have seen him get all excited when I rubbed some cream on his arm. Oh, he wanted me to rub more." She swayed back and forth. "I told him I have always been looking for a man like him. You can only imagine my surprise when he told me he wanted to marry me and leave me the fortune he got from playing the stock market." Her eyes hooded. "I told him I had a great lawyer, Emmitt Moss, who would discreetly change his will before we got married."

I glanced over at Junior. He hung his head in shame.

"What?" he chimed in when he looked up and saw the look on my face. "I'm still a man that believed in love."

"That's all it took, besides a couple weeks of him using my cream." Tinsie screwed the lid on the jar.

I wanted to jump up and grab her, but there was too much distance between us. She would have the gun in her hand and the trigger pulled before I got halfway there.

A cell phone chirped out a typewriter ringtone. A ringtone I knew well . . . Fluggie Callahan's.

"Oh God," I cried out and flung my head back. "You are the one who tried to kill Fluggie. And you took her phone?" Tears streamed down my face.

"Too bad she keeps all her notes on her phone and no one is ever going to read them." An evil grin pressed on Tinsie's lips.

My tears wouldn't stop no matter how hard I tried to mentally stop them. They were tears of hate-filled anger. It was more than personal. Everyone I had come in contact with was on Tinsie's death list.

"What about my granny and that plaster you

gave her?" I asked. My stomach knotted in fear at her answer.

The thought of me not having my granny was too much to bear. I wanted Tinsie to shoot me now.

"Just kill me! Kill me now!" I screamed at the top of my lungs.

A shot rang out. I crunched down and squeezed my eyes shut. A loud ringing beat in my ear. When I realized it was the sound of my heart beating loud, I squinted. Gun smoke hung in the air, parting a little. Like an angel, Dixie Dunn stood over the top of her own daughter, pointing a gun directly at Tinsie Dunn.

Chapter 26

"Do you think you are going to be okay?" Jack Henry grabbed the last box out of Charlotte Rae's office.

"Yeah." I smiled on the outside, but my insides were aching. I still couldn't believe Charlotte had taken the job at Hardgrove, even after she knew about the deal I had with the clients of Happy Times Retirement Community.

Jack Henry stood next to me, holding the box and looking at my face.

"New beginnings," I assured him. "Plus I might be able to talk freely to my Betweener clients."

"Let's hope you don't have any more of those." He kissed my cheek. "I'm going to put this in the moving truck, then I'll meet you over at the Inn?"

"Yeah." I plopped down behind the empty desk in what used to be Charlotte's chair. "I'm going to sit here for a minute and look around. You know," I hesitated. "I always wanted this to be my office."

"And you look beautiful in it." Jack Henry darted out the door.

I leaned way back in the chair and propped my feet up. It was the first time I had been alone since the takedown of Tinsie Dunn at Mamie Sue's house.

I felt sorry for Dixie Dunn. She hadn't known her real momma was Mamie Sue. Tinsie had told Jack Henry how she had overheard Pattie Dunn talking with Mamie Sue Preston. Actually, they'd been arguing. Mamie Sue had had one sexual encounter with Eugene Brown—Pastor Brown—before he'd left for seminary school. That one encounter had gotten Mamie pregnant with Dixie.

Mamie's parents hadn't allowed her to keep the baby, and they'd sent her away to work on part of their coal mine business on the clear other side of Kentucky. Mamie had been smart and had kept in touch with Pattie Dunn throughout the years.

Pattie hadn't had a lot of money, but Mamie had. So Mamie had paid for all of Pattie's needs. When Dixie had ended up pregnant, like her real momma, Pattie had made Dixie get a job cleaning houses. Dixie had been good at making home-made creams and facials, since they hadn't had a lot of money, and she'd begun to make the moisturizer on the side.

Pattie had still refused to tell Dixie about her real momma, and that was the conversation Tinsie had overheard. Tinsie had had Emmitt Moss look into it. She and Emmitt had hit it off after coming to an agreement about the millions of dollars Mamie Sue had had.

With Pattie Dunn out of the way, Dixie Dunn had been able to work for whomever she'd wanted, including Mamie Sue Preston, who'd been in dire need of a housekeeper.

It had been great for Mamie. Her daughter had finally been under her own roof. She'd even had her will changed to give everything to Dixie, except for the million dollars she'd given the church. Tinsie had never understood why Mamie never told Dixie about who she was. Waiting on the money, Tinsie and Emmitt had started to get antsy.

That was when they'd devised the plan to put arsenic in the moisturizer Dixie had made for Mamie. Little by little, Mamie had gotten sicker and sicker. It hadn't been enough arsenic to show on an autopsy. Emmitt and Tinsie had perfected the dose.

It had been bonus money, with all the properties Mamie had owned.

"You got it all figured out." Mamie sat on the edge of my new desk with her cane dangling off her thigh.

"Dixie is why you left the million dollars to the Sleepy Hollow Baptist Church?" I asked.

"Yes." She let out a long sigh and hopped off the desk. "I couldn't bring myself to tell Eugene I had his baby. I couldn't bring myself to date another man."

"He could've married you and helped you raise Dixie." I couldn't wrap my head around her reasoning.

"It was a different time back then. Ask your granny." Mamie smiled. "She was in love with Eugene. She hated it because he was in love with me. That's why she holds a grudge against me. It doesn't have anything to do with what funeral home buried me."

I could see Granny getting her panties all curled up about a man.

"Zula Fae and I were in competition all our lives. But look at her now." Mamie stood next to the window, looking out over the square.

The Inn was filled with people. Granny had forgiven Charlotte Rae and was giving her a going-away party. It was against my better judgment, but no one ever crossed Granny.

"My only regret was not telling Dixie I was her momma."

"Her eyes." I shook my head. "I swear she and Tinsie have Pastor Brown's eyes."

"Did you say my name?" Pastor Brown stood at my new office door.

"Pastor." I jumped up from the chair. "Do you like my new office?"

"I do." He smiled and walked in. Mamie Sue stood next to him. Her face lit up. She was obviously still in love. "I wanted to come by and thank you before I headed over to the Inn for the big party."

"Thank me for what?" I asked.

"For figuring out what really happened to Mamie Sue all those years ago." He didn't have to say much for me to know what he was talking about. "Now I know where the anonymous donation of one million dollars came from. I had my hunches, but I wasn't going to spend a dime of it. Thanks to Mamie, I can spend some money on updating the church and getting to know my daughter."

"You know about Dixie?" I asked.

"She can't deny she looks a lot like me." He

smiled. "I only wish Mamie would have come to me when it happened. Things would have been a lot different, and I would have been happy with it."

A tear slipped out of Mamie's eye and down her face.

"Can I make one suggestion?" I asked.

"Sure." He folded his arms.

"Maybe you should have some pew cushions made for those hard pews." I shrugged.

"I'll think about it. I'll see you at the party?" he asked.

"See you there." I waved 'bye.

When I saw him dart across the square, I knew it was safe to talk to Mamie.

"If it weren't for that smart boyfriend of yours, you might be dead too." Mamie reminded me of how Jack Henry had found us at Mamie's house.

After Dixie had shot her own daughter in the leg, she'd called the cops. Luckily, Jack Henry had been on to the murders, because Vernon Baxter had called him after the poison tests I had asked him to do had come back proving the moisturizer had been laced with arsenic.

Plus the hospital had told him Beulah had a case of arsenic poisoning. Unfortunately, Junior Mullins and Beulah were rich, and Tinsie and Emmitt had wanted more money. The more money they'd wanted, the greedier they'd gotten. Tinsie had only taken jobs with wealthy people. She'd had no plans to make Dixie Dunn's dreams of producing a moisturizer come true.

Now, with money in the bank and Tinsie in jail for the rest of her life, Dixie had decided to keep her cleaning company but move forward with the moisturizer company as well.

Poor Fluggie Callahan had been paid a visit by Emmitt Moss, leaving her bloody and beaten, but alive.

"You sure did good." Mamie turned back to the window and watched Eugene in the distance. "Now." She nodded her head and pointed her cane to the door. "We have some settling up to do."

"Settling up?" I asked.

"I told you I was paying you for helping me." She tilted her head for me to follow her.

"Don't you have the other side you need to get to?" I asked.

"Grab your hammer." She pointed to the hammer lying on the ground where Jack Henry and I had taken Charlotte Rae's things off the wall. "Hettie Bell is over at the Inn helping Zula, and we need to get into her studio."

What was one last gig with Mamie Sue Preston

going to hurt before she disappeared on me forever?

Junior Mullins had quickly passed over with Pattie Dunn once Tinsie had been discovered as the killer. It was how I knew the real killer had been found.

Pose and Relax was locked up tight. Mamie pointed to the window on the side of the building, the one facing the funeral home. It was pushed up a little, and I opened it a little more.

"Go on over and find that creaking board," Mamie instructed me.

The board that had mysteriously stopped creaking was creaking again.

"I made it creak when you were standing on it so you would know that is the board I want you to pull up and hammer back down," she said.

I bent down and did like she told me to. If I didn't, I was afraid she was going to stay on this side forever.

Once the board was up, I looked into the hole. There was an old paper bag. I took it out and looked in it.

"That's ten thousand dollars." Mamie stood over me. "It's yours. Don't tell no one."

"But I can't take your money. Someone will know." My mouth and eyes popped open.

"No one knows I put it there. I want you to have it. If you don't, I will haunt you forever," she warned. "You need help with the funeral-home bills, and that should help a little."

"Thank you so much, Mamie. But it is unnecessary. It's my job to help you get to the other side by seeking justice," I said, looking back at her.

It was too late. She was gone.

Chapter 27

So you think you can do this alone?" Charlotte Rae elbowed me.

"Think?" I let out a puff of air. "I know I can, and I can do it better."

People milled around the Inn, eating and drinking all the delicious food Granny had made.

"Hettie." I grabbed her arm to stop her when she went flying by with a few drinks in her hand to give to partygoers. "You need to go to Happy Times Retirement. They are wanting to get a yoga program for their residents there."

"Really?" she asked with excitement. "Then I can quit working for Zula Fae."

"No you can't." Granny moseyed up to us. "Go

take those drinks around before the ice melts,"
Granny warned Hettie.

"I'll look into it. Thanks, Emma Lee." She smiled
and worked her way through the crowd.

"Are you sure you want to do this?" Granny
asked Charlotte Rae.

"Yes," Charlotte and I said in unison. We let out
a big laugh.

Both of us seemed to be getting what we
wanted. Almost everything I wanted. I glanced
over at Jack Henry and his momma. They were
having a piece of Dixie Dunn's famous chess pie.

"Excuse me." I wanted to give Granny and
Charlotte some time alone, and I wanted to see
my boyfriend.

Beulah Paige and Fluggie were exchang-
ing war stories about Emmitt Moss and Tinsie
Dunn. They talked about the court date and
what they were going to say while they were on
the stand.

"There is our hero." Jo Francis held her glass
up to me and tilted her head to the side in a little
Southern toast.

"Yes, she is." Jack Henry pulled me tight. "Are
you okay?"

"I'm great." I smiled. "Fantastic."

"Well, I hate to bring this up here," Jo Francis

said, then she turned to Jack Henry. "Have you made a decision about your new job?"

"I'm so glad you asked, Mother." He took a deep breath. "I turned it down this morning."

Her face dropped. Her eyes bugged.

"Sleepy Hollow needs me. And I have to keep her out of trouble." He draped his arm around my shoulder. "I love you," he said to me.

"I love you too," I said back to him. I grabbed a glass of champagne off Hettie Bell's tray when she walked by. "Can I have everyone's attention please?" I yelled into the air.

The room fell silent, even the sound of the squeaking screen door. Once everyone was jammed into the Inn, I knew it was time.

"I wanted to take this opportunity to wish Charlotte Rae a happy new beginning of her life," I began my toast.

Even though Charlotte Rae and I never saw eye-to-eye, she was still my sister. After all, family was like fudge, sweet with a few nuts.

A GHOSTLY UNDERTAKING

A funeral, a ghost, a murder . . . It's all in a day's work for Emma Lee Raines. . . .

Bopped on the head from a falling plastic Santa, local undertaker Emma Lee Raines is told she's suffering from "funeral trauma." It's trauma all right, because the not-so-dearly departed keep talking to her. Take Ruthie Sue Payne—innkeeper, gossip queen, and arch-nemesis of Emma Lee's granny—she's adamant that she didn't just fall down those stairs. She was pushed.

Ruthie has no idea who wanted her pushing up daisies. All she knows is that she can't cross over until the matter is laid to eternal rest. In the land of the living, Emma Lee's high-school crush, Sheriff Jack Henry Ross, isn't ready to rule out foul play. Granny Raines, the widow of Ruthie's ex-husband and co-owner of the Sleepy Hollow Inn, is the prime suspect. Now Emma Lee is stuck playing detective or risk being haunted forever.

Another day. Another funeral. Another ghost.

Great. As if people didn't think I was freaky enough. But, truthfully, this was becoming a common occurrence for me as the director of Eternal Slumber Funeral Home.

Well, the funeral thing was common.

The ghost thing . . . that was new, making Sleepy Hollow anything *but* sleepy.

"What is *she* doing here?" A ghostly Ruthie Sue Payne stood next to me in the back of her own funeral, looking at the long line of Sleepy Hollow's residents that had come to pay tribute to her life. "I couldn't stand her while I was living, much less dead."

Ruthie, the local innkeeper, busybody and my

granny's arch-nemesis, had died two days ago after a fall down the stairs of her inn.

I hummed along to the tune of "Blessed Assurance," which was piping through the sound system, to try and drown out Ruthie's voice as I picked at baby's breath in the pure white blossom funeral spray sitting on the marble-top pedestal table next to the casket. The more she talked, the louder I hummed and rearranged the flowers, gaining stares and whispers of the mourners in the viewing room.

I was getting used to those stares.

"No matter how much you ignore me, I know you can hear and see me." Ruthie rested her head on my shoulder, causing me to nearly jump out of my skin. "If I'd known you were a light seeker, I probably would've been a little nicer to you while I was living."

I doubted that. Ruthie Sue Payne hadn't been the nicest lady in Sleepy Hollow, Kentucky. True to her name, she was a pain. Ruthie had been the president and CEO of the gossip mill. It didn't matter if the gossip was true or not, she told it.

Plus, she didn't care much for my family. Especially not after my granny married Ruthie's ex-husband, Earl. And *especially* not after Earl died and left Granny his half of the inn he and Ruthie had owned together . . . the inn where Granny and Ruthie both lived. The inn where Ruthie had died.

I glared at her. Well, technically I glared at Pastor Brown, because he was standing next to me and he obviously couldn't see Ruthie standing between us. Honestly, I wasn't sure there was a ghost between us, either. It had been suggested that the visions I had of dead people were hallucinations . . .

I kept telling myself that I was hallucinating, because it seemed a lot better than the alternative—I could see ghosts, talk to ghosts, be touched by ghosts.

"Are you okay, Emma Lee?" Pastor Brown laid a hand on my forearm. The sleeve on his brown pin-striped suit coat was a little too small, hitting above his wrist bone, exposing a tarnished metal watch. His razor-sharp blue eyes made his coal-black greasy comb-over stand out.

"Yes." I lied. "I'm fine." Fine as a girl who was having a ghostly hallucination could be.

"Are you sure?" Pastor Brown wasn't the only one concerned. The entire town of Sleepy Hollow had been worried about my well-being since my run-in with Santa Claus.

No, the spirit of Santa Claus hadn't visited me. *Yet*. Three months ago, a plastic Santa had done me in.

It was the darndest thing, a silly accident.

I abandoned the flower arrangement and smoothed a wrinkle in the thick velvet drapes, remembering that fateful day. The sun had been out, melting away the last of the Christmas snow. I'd decided to walk over to Artie's Meats and Deli, over on Main Street, a block away from the funeral home, to grab a bite for lunch since they had the best homemade chili this side of the Mississippi. I'd just opened the door when the snow and ice around the plastic Santa Claus Artie had put on the roof of the deli gave way, sending the five-foot jolly man crashing down on my head, knocking me out.

Flat out.

I knew I was on my way to meet my maker when Chicken Teater showed up at my hospital bedside. I had put Chicken Teater in the ground two years ago. But there he was, telling me all sorts of crazy things that I didn't understand. He blabbed on and on about guns, murders and all sorts of dealings I wanted to know nothing about.

It wasn't until my older sister and business partner, Charlotte Rae Raines, walked right through Chicken Teater's body, demanding that the doctor do something for my hallucinations, that I realized I wasn't dead after all.

I had been *hallucinating*. That's all. Hallucinating.

Doc Clyde said I had a case of the "Funeral Trauma" from working with the dead too long.

Too long? At twenty-eight, I had been an undertaker for only three years. I had been around the funeral home my whole life. It was the family business, currently owned by my granny, but run by my sister and me.

Some family business.

Ruthie tugged my sleeve, bringing me out of my memories. "And her!" she said, pointing across the room. Every single one of Ruthie's fingers was filled up to its knuckles with rings. She had been very specific in her funeral "pre-need" arrangements, and had diagramed where she wanted every single piece of jewelry placed on her during her viewing. The jewelry jangled as she wagged a finger at Sleepy Hollow's mayor, Anna Grace May. "I've been trying to get an appointment to see her for two weeks and she couldn't make time for me. Hmmph."

Doc Clyde had never been able to explain the touching thing. If Ruthie *was* a hallucination, how could she touch me? I rubbed my arm, trying to erase the feeling, and watched as everyone in the room turned their heads toward Mayor May.

Ruthie crossed her arms, lowered her brow and snarled. "Must be an election year, her showing up here like this."

"She's pretty busy," I whispered.

Mayor May sashayed her way up to see old Ruthie laid out, shaking hands along the way as if she were the president of the United States about to deliver the State of the Union speech. Her long, straight auburn hair was neatly tucked behind each ear, and her tight pencil skirt showed off her curvy body in just the right places. Her perfect white teeth glistened in the dull funeral-home setting.

If she wasn't close enough to shake your hand, the mayor did her standard wink and wave. I swear that was how she got elected. Mayor May was the first Sleepy Hollow official to ever get elected to office without being born and bred here. She was a quick talker and good with the old people, who made up the majority of the population. She didn't know the history of all the familial generations—how my grandfather had built Eternal Slumber with his own hands or how Sleepy Hollow had been a big coal town back in the day—which made her a bit of an outsider. Still, she was a good mayor and everyone seemed to like her.

All the men in the room eyed Mayor May's wiggle as she made her way down the center aisle of the viewing room. A few smacks could be heard from the women punching their husbands in the arm to stop them from gawking.

Ruthie said, "I know, especially now with that new development happening in town. It's why I wanted to talk to her."

New development? This was the first time I had heard anything about a new development. There hadn't been anything new in Sleepy Hollow in . . . a long time.

We could certainly use a little developing, but it would come at the risk of disturbing Sleepy Hollow's main income. The town was a top destination in Kentucky because of our many caves and caverns. Any digging could wreak havoc with what was going on underground.

Before I could ask Ruthie for more information, she said, "It's about time *they* got here."

In the vestibule, all the blue-haired ladies from the Auxiliary Club (Ruthie's only friends) stood side by side with their pocketbooks hooked in the crooks of their elbows. They were taking their sweet time signing the guest book.

The guest book was to be given to the next of kin, whom I still hadn't had any luck finding. As a matter of fact, I didn't have any family members listed in my files for Ruthie.

Ruthie walked over to her friends, eyeing them as they talked about her. She looked like she was chomping at the bit to join in the gossip, but put her hand up to her mouth. The corners of her eyes turned down, and a tear balanced on the edge of her eyelid as if she realized her fate had truly been sealed.

A flash of movement caught my eye, and I nearly groaned as I spotted my sister Charlotte Rae snaking through the crowd, her fiery gaze leveled on me. I tried to sidestep around Pastor Brown but was quickly jerked to a stop when she called after me.

"Did I just see you over here talking to yourself, Emma Lee?" She gave me a death stare that might just put me next to old Ruthie in her casket.

"Me? No." I laughed. When it came to Charlotte Rae, denial was my best defense.

My sister stood much taller than me. Her sparkly green eyes, long red hair, and girl-next-door look made families feel comfortable discussing their loved one's final resting needs with her. That was why she ran the sales side of our business, while I covered almost everything else.

Details. That was my specialty. I couldn't help

but notice Charlotte Rae's pink nails were a perfect match to her pink blouse. She was perfectly beautiful.

Not that I was unattractive, but my brown hair was definitely dull if I didn't get highlights, which reminded me that I needed to make an appointment at the hair salon. My hazel eyes didn't twinkle like Charlotte Rae's. Nor did my legs climb to the sky like Charlotte's. She was blessed with Grandpa Raines's family genes of long and lean, while I took after Granny's side of the family— average.

Charlotte Rae leaned over and whispered, "Seriously, are you seeing something?"

I shook my head. There was no way I was going to spill the beans about seeing Ruthie. Truth be told, I'd been positive that seeing Chicken Teater while I was in the hospital *had* been a figment of my imagination . . . until I was called to pick up Ruthie's dead body from the Sleepy Hollow Inn and Antiques, Sleepy Hollow's one and only motel.

When she started talking to me, there was no denying the truth.

I wasn't hallucinating.

I could see ghosts.

I hadn't quite figured out what to do with this

newfound talent of mine, and didn't really want to discuss it with anyone until I did. Especially Charlotte. If she suspected what was going on, she'd have Doc Clyde give me one of those little pills that he said cured the "Funeral Trauma," but only made me sleepy and groggy.

Charlotte Rae leaned over and fussed at me through her gritted teeth. "If you are seeing something or *someone*, you better keep your mouth shut."

That was one thing Charlotte Rae was good at. She could keep a smile on her face and stab you in the back at the same time. She went on. "You've already lost Blue Goose Moore and Shelby Parks to Burns Funeral Home because they didn't want the 'Funeral Trauma' to rub off on them."

My lips were as tight as bark on a tree about seeing or hearing Ruthie. In fact, I didn't understand enough of it myself to speak of it.

I was saved from more denials as the Auxiliary women filed into the viewing room one by one. I jumped at the chance to make them feel welcome—and leave my sister behind. "Right this way, ladies." I gestured down the center aisle for the Auxiliary women to make their way to the casket.

One lady shook her head. "I can't believe she

fell down the inn's steps. She was always so good on her feet. So sad."

"It could happen to any of us," another blue-haired lady rattled off as she consoled her friend.

"Yes, it's a sad day," I murmured and followed them up to the front of the room, stopping a few times on the way so they could say hi to some of the townsfolk they recognized.

"Fall?" Ruthie leaned against her casket as the ladies paid their respects. "What does she mean 'fall'?" Ruthie begged to know. Frantically, she looked at me and back at the lady.

I ignored her, because answering would really set town tongues to wagging, and adjusted the arrangement of roses that lay across the mahogany casket. The smell of the flowers made my stomach curl. There was a certain odor to a roomful of floral arrangements that didn't sit well with me. Even as a child, I never liked the scent.

Ruthie, however, was not going to be ignored.

"Emma Lee Raines, I know you can hear me. You listen to me." There was a desperate plea in her voice. "I didn't fall."

Okay, *that* got my attention. I needed to hear this. I gave a sharp nod of my chin, motioning for her to follow me.

Pulling my hands out of the rose arrangement,

I smoothed down the front of my skirt and started to walk back down the aisle toward the entrance of the viewing room.

We'd barely made it into the vestibule before Ruthie was right in my face. "Emma Lee, I did *not* fall down those stairs. Someone pushed me. Don't you understand? I was murdered!"

A GHOSTLY GRAVE

**There's a ghost on the loose—
and a fox in the henhouse**

Four years ago, the Eternal Slumber Funeral Home put Chicken Teater in the ground. Now undertaker Emma Lee Raines is digging him back up. The whole scene is bad for business, especially with her granny running for mayor and a big festival setting up in town. But ever since Emma Lee started seeing ghosts, Chicken's been pestering her to figure out who killed him.

With her handsome boyfriend, Sheriff Jack Henry Ross, busy getting new forensics on the old corpse, Emma Lee has time to look into her first suspect. Chicken's widow may be a former Miss Kentucky, but the love of his life was another beauty queen: Lady Cluckington, his prize-winning hen. Was Mrs. Teater the jealous type? Chicken seems to think so. Something's definitely rotten in Sleepy Hollow—and Emma Lee just prays it's not her luck.

Just think, this all started because of Santa Claus. I took a drink of my large Diet Coke Big Gulp that I had picked up from the Buy and Fly gas station on the way over to Sleepy Hollow Cemetery to watch Chicken Teater's body being exhumed from his eternal resting place—only he was far from restful.

Damn Santa. I sucked up a mouthful of Diet Coke and swallowed. *Damn Santa.*

No, I didn't mean the real jolly guy with the belly shaking like a bowlful of jelly who leaves baby dolls and toy trucks; I meant the plastic light-up ornamental kind that people stick in their front yards during Christmas. The particular plastic Santa I was talking about was the one that had fallen off the roof of Artie's Deli and Meat just as I happened to walk under it, knocking me flat out cold.

Santa didn't give me anything but a bump on the head and the gift of seeing ghosts—let me be more specific—ghosts of people who have been murdered. They called me the Betweener medium, at least that was what the psychic from Lexington told us . . . *us* . . . *sigh* . . . I looked over at Jack Henry.

The Ray Ban sunglasses covered up his big brown eyes, which were the exact same color as a Hershey's chocolate bar. I looked into his eyes. And as with a chocolate bar, once I stared at them, I was a goner. Lost, in fact.

Today I was positive his eyes would be watering from the stench of a casket that had been buried for four years—almost four years to the day, now that I thought about it.

Jack Henry, my boyfriend and Sleepy Hollow sheriff, motioned for John Howard Lloyd to drop the claw that was attached to the tractor and begin digging. John Howard, my employee at Eternal Slumber Funeral Home, didn't mind digging up the grave. He dug it four years ago, so why not? He hummed a tune, happily chewing—gumming, since he had no teeth—a piece of straw he had grabbed up off the ground before he took his post behind the tractor controls. If someone who didn't know him came upon John Howard, they'd think he was a serial killer, with his dirty overalls, wiry hair and gummy smile.

The buzz of a moped scooter caused me to look back at the street. There was a crowd that had gathered behind the yellow police line to see what was happening because it wasn't every day someone's body was plucked from its resting place.

"Zula Fae Raines Payne, get back here!" an officer scolded my granny, who didn't pay him any attention. She waved her handkerchief in the air with one hand while she steered her moped right on through the police tape. "This is a crime scene and you aren't allowed over there."

Granny didn't even wobble but held the moped steady when she snapped right through the yellow tape.

"Woo hoooo, Emma!" Granny hollered, ignoring the officer, who was getting a little too close to her. A black helmet snapped on the side covered the top of her head, giving her plenty of room to sport her large black-rimmed sunglasses. She twisted the handle to full throttle. The officer took off at a full sprint to catch up to her. He put his arm out to grab her. "I declare!" Granny jerked her head back. "I'm Zula Raines Payne, the owner of Eternal Slumber, and this is one of my clients!"

"Ma'am, I know who you are. With all due respect, because my momma and pa taught me to respect my elders—and I do respect you, Ms. Payne—I can't let you cross that tape. You are going to have to go back behind the line!" He ran behind her and pointed to the yellow tape that she had already zipped through. "This is a crime scene. Need I remind you that you turned over operations of your business to your granddaughter? And only *she* has the right to be on the other side of the line."

I curled my head back around to see what Jack Henry and John were doing and pretended the roar of the excavator was drowning out the sounds around me, including those of Granny screaming my name. Plus, I didn't want to get into any sort of argument with Granny, since half the town came out to watch the 7 a.m. exhumation, and the Auxiliary women were the first in line—and would be the first to be at the Higher Grounds Café, eating their scones, drinking their coffee and coming up with all sorts of reasons why we had exhumed the body.

I could hear them now. *Ever since Zula Fae left Emma Lee and Charlotte Rae in charge of Eternal*

Slumber, it's gone downhill, or my personal favorite, *I'm not going to lay my corpse at Eternal Slumber just to have that crazy Emma Lee dig me back up. Especially since she's got a case of the Funeral Trauma.*

The "Funeral Trauma." After the whole Santa incident, I told Doc Clyde I was having some sort of hallucinations and seeing dead people. He said I had been in the funeral business a little too long and seeing corpses all of my life had been traumatic.

Regardless, the officer was half right—me and my sister were in charge of Eternal Slumber. At twenty-eight, I had been an undertaker for only three years. But, I had been around the funeral home my whole life. It is the family business, one I didn't want to do until I turned twenty-five years old and decided I better keep the business going. *Some business.* Currently, Granny still owned Eternal Slumber, but my sister, Charlotte Rae, and I ran the joint.

My parents completely retired and moved to Florida. Thank God for Skype or I'd never see them. I guess Granny was semi-retired. I say semi-retired because she put her two cents in when she wanted to. Today she wanted to.

Some family business.

Granny brought the moped to an abrupt stop.

She hopped right off and flicked the snap of the strap and pulled the helmet off along with her sunglasses. She hung the helmet on the handlebars and the glasses dangled from the *V* in her sweater exactly where she wanted it to hang—between her boobs. Doc Clyde was there and Granny had him on the hook exactly where she wanted to keep him.

Her short flaming-red hair looked like it was on fire, with the morning sun beaming down as she used her fingers to spike it up a little more than usual. After all, she knew she had to look good because she was the center of attention—next to Chicken Teater's exhumed body.

The officer ran up and grabbed the scooter's handle. He knew better than to touch Granny.

"I am sure your momma and pa did bring you up right, but if you don't let me go . . ." Granny jerked the scooter toward her. She was a true Southern belle and put things in a way that no other woman could. I looked back at them and waved her over. The police officer stepped aside. Granny took her hanky out of her bra and wiped off the officer's shoulder like she was cleaning lint or something. "It was *lovely* to meet you." Granny's voice dripped like sweet honey. She put the hanky back where she had gotten it.

I snickered. *Lovely* wasn't always a compliment from a Southern gal. Like the gentleman he claimed to be, he took his hat off to Granny and smiled.

She didn't pay him any attention as she beelined it toward me.

"Hi," she said in her sweet Southern drawl, waving at everyone around us. She gave a little extra wink toward Doc Clyde. His cheeks rose to a scarlet red. Nervously, he ran his fingers through his thinning hair and pushed it to the side, defining the side part.

Everyone in town knew he had been keeping late hours just for Granny, even though she wasn't a bit sick. God knew what they were doing and I didn't want to know.

Granny pointed her hanky toward Pastor Brown who was there to say a little prayer when the casket was exhumed. Waking the dead wasn't high on anyone's priority list. Granny put the cloth over her mouth and leaning in, she whispered, "Emma Lee, you better have a good reason to be digging up Chicken Teater."

We both looked at the large concrete chicken gravestone. The small gold plate at the base of the stone statue displayed all of Colonel Chicken Teater's stats with his parting words: *Chicken has left the coop.*

"Why don't you go worry about the Inn." I suggested for her to leave and glanced over at John Howard. He had to be getting close to reaching the casket vault.

Granny gave me the stink-eye.

"It was only a suggestion." I put my hands up in the air as a truce sign.

Granny owned, operated and lived at the only bed-and-breakfast in town, the Sleepy Hollow Inn, known as "the Inn" around here. Everyone loved staying at the large mansion, which sat at the foothills of the caverns and caves that made Sleepy Hollow a main attraction in Kentucky . . . besides horses and University of Kentucky basketball.

Sleepy Hollow was a small tourist town that was low on crime, and that was the way we liked it.

Sniff, sniff. Whimpers were coming from underneath the large black floppy hat.

Granny and I looked over at Marla Maria Teater, Chicken's wife. She had come dressed to the nines with her black V-neck dress hitting her curves in all the right places. The hat covered up the eyes she was dabbing.

Of course, when the police notified her that they had good reason to believe that Chicken didn't die of a serious bout of pneumonia but was murdered, Marla took to her bed as any mourning widower would. She insisted on being here for the exhumation. Jack Henry had warned Marla Maria to keep quiet about why the police were opening up the files on Chicken's death. If there was a murderer on the loose and it got around, it could possibly hurt the economy, and this was Sleepy Hollow's busiest time of the year.

Granny put her arm around Marla and winked at me over Marla's shoulder.

"Now, now. I know it's hard, honey, I've buried a few myself. Granted, I've never had any dug up though." Granny wasn't lying. She has been twice widowed and I was hoping she'd stay away from marriage a third time. Poor Doc Clyde, you'd have thought he would stay away from her since her track record was . . . well . . . deadly. "That's a first in this town." Granny gave Marla Maria the elbow along with a wink and a click of her tongue.

Maybe the third time was the charm.

"Who is buried here?" Granny let go of Marla and stepped over to the smaller tombstone next to Chicken's.

"Stop!" Jack Henry screamed, waving his hands in the air. "Zula, move!"

Granny looked up and ducked just as John

Howard came back for another bite of ground with the claw.

I would hate to have to bury Granny anytime soon.

"Lady Cluckington," Marla whispered, tilting her head to the side. Using her finger, she dabbed the driest eyes I had ever seen. "Our prize chicken. Well, she isn't dead *yet*."

I glanced over at her. Her tone caused a little suspicion to stir in my gut.

"She's not a chicken. She's a Spangled Russian Orloff Hen!" Chicken Teater appeared next to his grave. His stone looked small next to his six-foot-two frame. He ran his hand over the tombstone Granny had asked about. There was a date of birth, but no date of death. "You couldn't stand having another beauty queen in my life!"

"Oh no," I groaned and took another gulp of my Diet Coke. He—his ghost—was the last thing that I needed to see this morning.

"Is that sweet tea?" Chicken licked his lips. "I'd give anything to have a big ole sip of sweet tea." He towered over me. His hair was neatly combed to the right; his red plaid shirt was tucked into his carpenter jeans.

This was the third time I had seen Chicken Teater since his death. It was a shock to the community to hear of a man passing from pneumonia in his early sixties. But that was what the doctors in Lexington said he died of, no questions asked, and his funeral was held at Eternal Slumber.

The first time I had seen Chicken Teater's ghost was after my perilous run-in with Santa. I too thought I was a goner, gone to the great beyond . . . but no . . . Chicken Teater and Ruthie Sue Payne— their ghosts anyway—stood right next to my hospital bed, eyeballing me. Giving me the onceover as if he was trying to figure out if I was dead or alive. Lucky for him I was alive and seeing him.

Ruthie Sue Payne was a client at Eternal Slumber who couldn't cross over until someone helped her solve her murder. That someone was me. The Betweener.

Since I could see her, talk to her, feel her and hear her, I was the one. Thanks to me, Ruthie's murder was solved and she was now resting peacefully on the other side. Chicken was a different story.

Apparently, Ruthie was as big of a gossip in the afterlife as she was in her earthly life. That was how Chicken Teater knew about me being a Betweener. Evidently, Ruthie was telling everyone about my special gift.

Chicken Teater wouldn't leave me alone until I agreed to investigate his death because he knew he didn't die from pneumonia. He claimed he was poisoned. But who would want to kill a chicken farmer?

Regardless, it took several months of me trying to convince Jack Henry there might be a possibility Chicken Teater was murdered. After some questionable evidence, provided by Chicken Teater, the case was reopened. I didn't understand all the red tape and legal yip-yap, but here we stood today.

Now it was time for me to get Chicken Teater to the other side.

"It's not dead yet?" Granny's eyebrows rose in amazement after Marla Maria confirmed there was an empty grave. Granny couldn't get past the fact there was a gravestone for something that wasn't dead.

I was still stuck on "prize chicken." What was a prize chicken?

A loud thud echoed when John Howard sent the claw down. There was an audible gasp from the crowd. The air was thick with anticipation. What did they think they were going to see?

Suddenly my nerves took a downward dive. What if the coffin opened? Coffin makers guaranteed they lock for eternity after they are sealed, but still, it wouldn't be a good thing for John Howard to pull the coffin up and have Chicken take a tumble next to Lady Cluckington's stone.

"I think we got 'er!" John Howard stood up in the cab of the digger with pride on his face as he looked down in the hole. "Yep! That's it!" he hollered over the roar of the running motor.

Jack Henry ran over and hooked some cables on the excavator and gave the thumbs-up.

Pastor Brown dipped his head and moved his lips in a silent prayer. Granny nudged me with her boney elbow to bow my head, and I did. Marla Maria cried out.

"Aw shut up!" Chicken Teater told her and smiled as he saw his coffin being raised from the earth. "They are going to figure out who killed me, and so help me, if it was you . . ." He shook his fist in the air in Marla Maria's direction.

Curiosity stirred in my bones. Was it going to be easy getting Chicken Teater to the other side? Was Marla Maria Teater behind his death as Chicken believed?

She was the only one who was not only in his bed at night, but right by his deathbed, so he told me. I took my little notebook out from my back pocket. I had learned from Ruthie's investigation to never leave home without it. I jotted down what Chicken had said to Marla Maria, with prize chickens next to it, followed up by a lot of exclamation points. Oh . . . I had almost forgotten that Marla Maria was Miss Kentucky in her earlier years—a *beauty queen*—I quickly wrote that down too.

"Are you getting all of this?" Chicken questioned me and twirled his finger in a circle as he referred to the little scene Marla Maria was causing with her meltdown. She leaned her butt up against Lady Cluckington's stone. Chicken rushed over to his prize chicken's gravestone and tried to shove Marla Maria off. "Get your—"

Marla Maria jerked like she could feel something touch her. She shivered. Her body shimmied from her head to her toes.

I cleared my throat, doing my best to get Chicken to stop fusing and cursing. "Are you okay?" I asked. Did she feel him?

Granny stood there taking it all in.

Marla crossed her arms in front of her and ran her hands up and down them. "I guess when I buried Chicken, I thought that was the end of it. This is creeping me out a little bit."

End of it? End of what? Your little murder plot? My mind unleashed all sorts of ways Marla Maria might have offed her man. That seemed a little too suspicious for me. Marla buttoned her lip when Jack Henry walked over. More suspicious behavior that I duly noted.

"Can you tell me how he died?" I put a hand on her back to offer some comfort, though I knew she was putting on a good act.

She shook her head, dabbed her eye and said, "He was so sick. Coughing and hacking. I was so mad because I had bags under my eyes from him keeping me up at night." *Sniff, sniff.* "I had to dab some Preparation H underneath my eyes in order to shrink them." She tapped her face right above her cheekbones.

"That's where my butt cream went?" Chicken hooted and hollered. "She knew I had a hemorrhoid the size of a golf ball and she used my cream on her face?" Chicken flailed his arms around in the air.

I bit my lip and stepped a bit closer to Marla Maria so I couldn't see Chicken out of my peripheral vision. There were a lot of things I had heard in my time, but hemorrhoids were something that I didn't care to know about.

I stared at Marla Maria's face. There wasn't a tear, a tear streak, or a single wrinkle on her perfectly made-up face. If hemorrhoids helped shrink her under-eye bags, did it also help shrink her wrinkles?

"Anyway, enough about me." She fanned her face with the handkerchief. "Chicken was so uncomfortable with all the phlegm. He could barely breathe. I let him rest, but called the doctor in the meantime." She nodded and waited for me to agree with her. I nodded back and she continued. "When the doctor came out of the bedroom, he told me Chicken was dead." A cry burst out of her as she threw her head back and held the hanky over her face.

I was sure she was hiding a smile from thinking she was pulling one over on me. Little did she know this wasn't my first rodeo with a murderer. Still, I patted her back while Chicken spat at her feet.

Jack Henry walked over. He didn't take his eyes off of Marla Maria.

"I'm sorry we have to do this, Marla." Jack took his hat off out of respect for the widow. *Black widow*, I thought as I watched her fidget side to side, avoiding all eye contact by dabbing the corners of her eyes. "We are all done here, Zula." He nodded toward Granny.

Granny smiled.

Marla Maria nodded before she turned to go face her waiting public behind the police line.

Granny walked over to say something to Doc Clyde, giving him a little butt pat and making his face even redder than before. I waited until she was out of earshot before I said something to Jack Henry.

"That was weird. Marla Maria is a good actress." I made mention to Jack Henry because sometimes he was clueless as to how women react to different situations.

"Don't be going and blaming her just because she's his wife." Jack Henry was trying to play the good cop he always was, but I wasn't falling for his act. "It's all speculation at this point."

"Wife? She was no kind of wife to me." Chicken kicked his foot in the dirt John Howard had dug from his grave. "She only did one thing as my wife." Chicken looked back and watched Marla Maria play the poor pitiful widow as Beulah Paige Bellefry, president and CEO of Sleepy Hollow's gossip mill, drew her into a big hug while all the other Auxiliary women gathered to put in their two cents.

"La-la-la." I put my fingers in my ears and tried to drown him out. I only wanted to know how he was murdered, not how Marla Maria *was* a wife to him.

"She spent all my money," he cursed under his breath.

"Shoo." I let out an audible sigh.

Over Jack's right shoulder, in the distance some movement caught my eye near the trailer park. There was a man peering out from behind a tree looking over at all the commotion. His John Deere hat helped shadow his face so I couldn't get a good look, but I chalked it up to being a curious neighbor like the rest of them. Still, I quickly wrote down the odd behavior. I had learned you never know what people knew. And I had to start from scratch on how to get Chicken to the great beyond. I wasn't sure, but I believe Chicken had lived in the trailer park. Maybe the person saw something, maybe not. He was going on the list.

"Are you okay?" Jack pulled off his sunglasses. His big brown eyes were set with worry. I grinned. A smile ruffled his mouth. "Just checking because of the la-la thing." He waved his hands in the air. "I saw you taking some notes and I know what that means."

"Yep." My one word confirmed that Chicken was there and spewing all sorts of valuable information. Jack Henry was the only person who knew I was a Betweener, and he knew Chicken was right here with us even though he couldn't see him. When I told him about Chicken Teater's little visits to me and how he wouldn't leave me alone until we figured out who killed him, Jack Henry knew it to be true. "I'll tell you later."

I jotted down a note about Marla Maria spending all of Chicken's money, or so he said. Which made me question her involvement even more. Was he no use to her with a zero bank account and she offed him? I didn't know he had money.

"I can see your little noggin running a mile a minute." Jack bent down and looked at me square in the eyes.

"Just taking it all in." I bit my lip. I had learned from my last ghost that I had to keep some things to myself until I got the full scoop. And right now, Chicken hadn't given me any solid information.

"You worry about getting all the information you can from your little friend." Jack Henry pointed to the air beside me. I pointed to the air beside him where Chicken's ghost was actually standing. Jack grimaced. "Whatever. I don't care where he is." He shivered.

Even though Jack Henry knew I could see ghosts, he wasn't completely comfortable.

"You leave the investigation to me." Jack Henry put his sunglasses back on. Sexy dripped from him, making my heart jump a few beats.

"Uh-huh." I looked away. Looking away from

Jack Henry when he was warning me was a common occurrence. I knew I had to do my own investigating and couldn't get lost in his eyes while lying to him.

Besides, I didn't have a whole lot of information. Chicken knew he was murdered but had no clue how. He was only able to give me clues about his life and it was up to me to put them together.

"I'm not kidding." Jack Henry took his finger and put it on my chin, pulling it toward him. He gave me a quick kiss. "We are almost finished up here. I'll sign all the paperwork and send the body on over to Eternal Slumber for Vernon to get going on some new toxicology reports we have ordered." He took his officer hat off and used his forearm to wipe the sweat off his brow.

"He's there waiting," I said. Vernon Baxter was a retired doctor who performed any and all autopsies the Sleepy Hollow police needed and I let him use Eternal Slumber for free. I had all the newest technology and equipment used in autopsies in the basement of the funeral home.

"Go on up!" Jack Henry gave John the thumbs-up and walked closer. Slowly John Howard lifted the coffin completely out of the grave and sat it right on top of the church truck, which looked like a gurney.

"Do you think she did it?" I glanced over at Marla Maria, as she talked a good talk.

"Did what?" Granny walked up and asked. She turned to see what I was looking at. "Did you dig him up because his death is being investigated for murder?" Granny gasped.

"Now Granny, don't go spreading rumors." I couldn't deny or admit to what she said. If I admitted the truth to her question, I would be betraying Jack Henry. If I denied her question, I would be lying to Granny. And no one lies to Granny.

In a lickety-split, Granny was next to her scooter.

"I'll be over. Put the coffee on," Granny hollered before she put her helmet back on her head, snapped the strap in place, and revved up the scooter and buzzed off in the direction of town, giving a little *toot-toot* and wave to the Auxiliary women as she passed.

Once the chains were unhooked from the coffin and the excavator was out of the way, Jack Henry and I guided the coffin on the church truck into the back of my hearse. Before I shut the door, I had a sick feeling that someone was watching me. Of course the crowd was still there, but I mean someone was watching *my* every move.

I looked back over my shoulder toward the trailer park. The man in the John Deere hat popped out of sight behind the tree when he saw me look at him.

I shut the hearse door and got into the driver's side. Before I left the cemetery, I looked in my rearview mirror at the tree. The man was standing there. This time the shadow of the hat didn't hide his eyes.

We locked eyes.

"Look away," Chicken Teater warned me when he appeared in the passenger seat.

A GHOSTLY DEMISE

**The prodigal father returns—
but this ghost is no holy spirit**

When she runs into her friend's deadbeat dad at the local deli, undertaker Emma Lee Raines can't wait to tell Mary Anna Hardy that he's back in Sleepy Hollow, Kentucky, after five long years. Cephus Hardy may have been the town drunk, but he didn't disappear on an epic bender like everyone thought: He was murdered. And he's heard that Emma Lee's been helping lost souls move on to that great big party in the sky.

Why do ghosts always bother Emma Lee at the worst times? Her granny's mayoral campaign is in high gear, a carnival is taking over the Town Square, and her hunky boyfriend, Sheriff Jack Henry Ross, is stuck wrestling runaway goats. Besides, Cephus has no clue whodunit . . . unless it was one of Mrs. Hardy's not-so-secret admirers. All roads lead Emma Lee to that carnival—and a killer who isn't clowning around.

Cephus Hardy?"

Stunned. My jaw dropped when I saw Cephus Hardy walk up to me in the magazine aisle of Artie's Meat and Deli. I was admiring the cover of *Cock and Feathers*, where my last client at Eternal Slumber Funeral Home, Chicken Teater, graced the cover with his prize Orloff Hen, Lady Cluckington.

"I declare." A Mack truck could've hit me and I wouldn't have felt it. I grinned from ear to ear.

Cephus Hardy looked the exact same as he did five years ago. Well, from what I could remember from his social visits with my momma and daddy and the few times I had seen him around our small town of Sleepy Hollow, Kentucky.

His tight, light brown curls resembled a baseball helmet. When I was younger, it amazed me how thick and dense his hair was. He always wore polyester taupe pants with the perfectly straight crease down the front, along with a brown belt. The hem of his pants ended right above the shoelaces in his white, patent-leather shoes. He tucked in his short-sleeved, plaid shirt, making it so taut you could see his belly button.

"Momma and Daddy live in Florida now, but they are going to be so happy when I tell them you are back in town. Everyone has been so worried about you." I smiled and took in his sharp, pointy nose and rosy red cheeks. I didn't take my eyes off him as I put the copy of *Cock and Feathers* back in the rack. I leaned on my full cart of groceries and noticed he hadn't even aged a bit. No wrinkles. Nothing. "Where the hell have you been?"

He shrugged. He rubbed the back of his neck.

"Who cares?" I really couldn't believe it. Mary Anna was going to be so happy since he had just up and left five years ago, telling no one—nor had he contacted anyone since. "You won't believe what Granny is doing."

I pointed over his shoulder at the election

poster taped up on Artie's Meat and Deli's storefront window.

"Granny is running against O'Dell Burns for mayor." I cackled, looking in the distance at the poster of Zula Fae Raines Payne all laid-back in the rocking chair on the front porch of the Sleepy Hollow Inn with a glass of her famous iced tea in her hand.

It took us ten times to get a picture she said was good enough to use on all her promotional items for the campaign. Since she was all of five-foot-four, her feet dangled. She didn't want people to vote on her size; therefore, the photo was from the lap up. I told Granny that I didn't know who she thought she was fooling. Everyone who was eligible to vote knew her and how tall she was. She insisted. I didn't argue anymore. No one, and I mean no one, wins an argument against Zula Fae Raines Payne. Including me.

"She looks good." Cephus raised his brows, lips turned down.

"She sure does," I noted.

For a twice-widowed seventy-seven-year-old, Granny acted like she was in her fifties. I wasn't sure if her red hair was still hers or if Mary Anna kept it up on the down-low, but Granny would never be seen going to Girl's Best Friend unless there was some sort of gossip that needed to be heard. Otherwise, she wanted everyone to see her as the good Southern belle she was.

"Against O'Dell Burns?" Cephus asked. Slowly, he nodded in approval.

It was no secret that Granny and O'Dell had butted heads a time or two. The outcome of the election was going to be interesting, to say the least.

"Yep. She retired three years ago, leaving me and Charlotte Rae in charge of Eternal Slumber."

It was true. I was the undertaker of Eternal Slumber Funeral Home. It might make some folks' skin crawl to think about being around dead people all the time, but it was job security at its finest. O'Dell Burns owned Burns Funeral, the other funeral home in Sleepy Hollow, which made him and Granny enemies from the get-go.

O'Dell didn't bother me though. Granny didn't see it that way. We needed a new mayor, and O'Dell stepped up to the plate at the council meeting, but Granny wouldn't hear of it. So the competition didn't stop with dead people; now Granny wants all the living people too. As mayor.

"Long story short," I rambled on and on, "Granny married Earl Way Payne. He died and left Granny the Sleepy Hollow Inn. I don't know what she is thinking running for mayor because she's so busy taking care of all of the tourists at the Inn. Which reminds me"—I planted my hands on my hips—"you never answered my question. Have you seen Mary Anna yet?"

"Not yet." His lips curved in a smile.

"She's done real good for herself. She opened Girl's Best Friend Spa and has all the business since she's the only one in town. And"—I wiggled my brows—"she is working for me at Eternal Slumber."

A shiver crawled up my spine and I did a little shimmy shake, thinking about her fixing the corpses' hair and makeup. Somebody had to do it and Mary Anna didn't seem to mind a bit.

I ran my hand down my brown hair that Mary Anna had recently dyed since my short stint as a blond. I couldn't do my own hair, much less someone else's. Same for the makeup department.

I never spent much time in front of the mirror. I worked with the dead and they weren't judging me.

"Emma Lee?" Doc Clyde stood at the end of the magazine aisle with a small shopping basket in the crook of his arm. His lips set in a tight line. "Are you feeling all right?"

"Better than ever." My voice rose when I pointed

to Cephus. "Especially now that Cephus is back in town."

"Have you been taking your meds for the Funeral Trauma?" He ran his free hand in his thin hair, placing the few remaining strands to the side. His chin was pointy and jutted out even more as he shuffled his thick-soled doctor shoes down the old, tiled floor. "You know, it's only been nine months since your accident. And it could take years before the symptoms go away."

"Funeral Trauma," I muttered, and rolled my eyes.

Cephus just grinned.

The Funeral Trauma.

A few months back I had a perilous incident with a plastic Santa Claus right here at Artie's Meat and Deli. I had walked down from the funeral home to grab some lunch. Artie had thought it was a good idea to put a life-sized plastic Santa on the roof. It was a good idea until the snow started melting and the damn thing slid right off the roof just as I was walking by, knocking me square out. Flat.

I woke up in the hospital seeing ghosts of the corpse I had buried six feet deep. I thought I had gone to the Great Beyond. But I could see my family and all the living.

I told Doc Clyde I was having some sort of hallucinations and seeing dead people. He said I had been in the funeral business a little too long and seeing corpses all of my life had been traumatizing. Granny had been in the business for over forty years. I had only been in the business for three. Something didn't add up.

Turned out, a psychic confirmed I am what was called a Betweener.

I could see ghosts of the dead who were stuck between the here and the after. Of course, no one but me and Jack Henry, my boyfriend and Sleepy Hollow's sheriff, knew. And he was still a little apprehensive about the whole thing.

"I'm fine," I assured Doc Clyde, and looked at Cephus. "Wait." I stopped and tried to swallow what felt like a mound of sand in my mouth. My mind hit rewind and took me back to the beginning of my conversation with Cephus.